BACKWARDS

BACKWARDS

BACKWARDS

TODD MITCHELL

CANDLEWICK PRESS

Copyright © 2013 by Todd Mitchell

First edition 2013

Library of Congress Catalog Card Number 2013931469
ISBN 978-0-7636-6277-6

13 14 15 16 17 18 BVG
1 2 3 4 5 6 7 8 9 10

Printed in Berryville, VA, U.S.A.

This book was typeset in Dante.

Candlewick Press
99 Dover Street
Somerville, Massachusetts 02144

visit us at www.candlewick.com

To anyone who's ever lived backwards, you are not alone.

Part I

Saturday, November 15

Bright-red tulips blooming—that's the first thing I remember. Only they weren't tulips. Their petals were drops of crimson, sinking into bathwater. It hit me that the drops must be coming from somewhere. Then I saw his wrists, and I realized that the red was blood. I didn't feel any revulsion or sadness. Instead, I was struck by how bright the drops swirling in the water looked. I wanted him to move his arms so there could be more pretty blossoms—a whole tub full of tulips, flashy as springtime—but he merely let his arms fall beneath the surface, coming to rest on his legs and turning the water pink. So much for art.

He wasn't naked. That seemed strange to me. He wore jeans and a T-shirt, and sneakers, all of which were soaked. It didn't look very comfortable — wearing wet jeans and shoes in a tub like that. He let his head rest on the porcelain edge, which also didn't look comfortable, and a small, rectangular blade slipped from his hand. Then he shifted, knocking several shampoo bottles over. His brow creased. Perhaps he wondered if he should pick up the mess, but he must have realized that his hands would drip blood onto the floor, so he left the bottles where they lay and closed his eyes.

Once he did that, I was able to get a little distance from him and hover above his body. If he was aware of my presence, he gave no sign of it. He was tall and gawky — too big for the tub, so his legs peaked like a child's drawing of mountains and his shoulders hunched. Pink water lapped halfway up his shirt, but his hair and face were still dry, and the knees of his jeans looked dry as well. I thought it must frustrate him not to be able to submerge his whole body in the warmth of the water. He seemed young — seventeen or eighteen — so it probably hadn't been that long ago when he'd been able to stretch out fully in the bathtub. I wondered if it surprised him when he discovered he didn't fit anymore.

An open bottle of aspirin lay beside the tub, and a

few white pills had spilled across the floor, dissolving in a puddle near the shampoo bottles. I pictured him downing a handful of aspirin before opening the package of razor blades. His sweatshirt was draped over the toilet seat like a tablecloth with two car keys resting in the center on a yellow sticky note. FOR TEAGAN the note said in blocky letters, slightly smeared.

He stirred and I felt a tug, as if I were a kite being jerked back to earth. He glanced through heavy lids at the pen on the edge of the sink. I didn't have much trouble guessing his thoughts—he wanted to write more on the note or write another, longer note. That's what he was supposed to do, right? Leave a note? But it was too late now because his shoes and jeans and shirt were already wet, and if he got out of the tub to get the pen and more paper, he'd drip pink puddles everywhere.

With a frustrated sigh, he lay back. Maybe he was crying, although I didn't see any tears. I had a hard time feeling sympathy for him. After all, what sort of person only leaves behind a sticky note with two smudged words and a set of keys? The whole scene really started to depress me. I tried to pull away and escape from the room, but I was yanked back again.

"What the hell, Dan!" called a girl's voice. The doorknob rattled. "Are you taking a bath? It's almost noon."

So the guy in the tub was named Dan. He struggled to lift one arm, but it flopped back into the water. His face looked as pale as the tile walls.

"I need to take my contacts out," continued the girl. "They itch."

Dan rolled his head from side to side and muttered a faint protest.

"Fine. Have it your way." The girl left, only to return a minute later to rattle the doorknob again. "You better not be naked," she warned.

After several seconds of rattling, the lock clicked and the door swung open. The girl stood in the doorway, holding the screwdriver she must have used to jimmy the lock.

Despite her dyed-black hair, slight frame, and pierced nose and eyebrow, the resemblance between her and Dan was striking. They both had high cheekbones and hazel eyes. Seeing his sister, I realized that Dan might be considered handsome, although right now he looked about as appealing as curdled milk.

The girl's expression darkened as she took in the scene. Dan's eyes had closed. If he was still conscious, he was doing his best not to look it.

"Very funny," muttered the girl. She must have thought Dan was pulling a prank on her. "If Mom saw you, she'd lose her shit." The girl shoved his shoulder, but he didn't respond. *"Dan?"* she said, faintly at first. "Dan. Dan!"

Her toughness came apart like tissue paper as it dawned on her that he wasn't faking. Then her face creased and her mouth twitched. I hated seeing her break down, but I couldn't leave. I couldn't even look away while she collapsed, uttering a fragmented prayer of "God" and "Mom" and "Please."

My sense of things got blurry after that. I saw Dan's mom arrive. She fought back her initial horror and attempted to pull her gawky son out of the tub, but she couldn't lift him. She finally settled for raising his arms out of the water and wrapping his wrists in towels. Her face looked brittle. In a way, her choked reaction bothered me more than the sister's cries.

"Call an ambulance," said the mom, but the girl didn't move. "Teagan, call an ambulance!" she repeated.

The girl still wouldn't move, so the mom went to get a phone herself. Her voice sounded strangely detached, as if she refused to accept what she was saying.

After stating the necessary details, the mom returned with yellow dish towels. Dan's wrists had slipped back into the water in her absence, and the bath towels were soaking wet. She wrapped the new towels around the old ones, but it did little to keep the blood in. Still, she held the wet towels tight to Dan's wrists until the ambulance arrived.

The paramedics rang the doorbell several times before the mom went to let them in. Teagan stayed in the bathroom, frozen. One of the paramedics, a tall guy with a shaved head, had to physically drag her out so they'd have room to work in the cramped space.

I watched them step into the tub and hoist up Dan's body. The tall paramedic banged his knee on the tub spout and cursed. Pink water splashed onto the bath rug and spilled across the floor into the white-carpeted hall. The mess was tremendous now. I felt myself growing angry at Dan for causing it. It wasn't simply the stains on the floor that upset me, but the way his actions would affect his mom and sister, staining their lives, too.

The paramedics lay his body on the floor. Then the shorter one jogged to the truck, tracking bloody water everywhere, while the tall one put tourniquets on Dan's arms, cut through his jeans, and attempted to insert an IV. He asked how many aspirin Dan had taken. No one knew the answer.

By this point, I had to struggle to stay focused, but I kept watching because of the mom and the sister. I wished I could do something for them.

The tall paramedic pushed a gurney into the hall, but he couldn't get it through the bathroom door. They had to drag Dan's body out to load him up. Then they strapped him on. I doubted he had much of a pulse anymore. His pale limbs jiggled as they rushed to wheel him to the ambulance.

Once outside, I tried to drift away. I wanted to float into the overcast sky and be free of this whole mess, but the images of what I'd seen became tight and heavy, tugging me back toward Dan. No matter how much I fought, I kept getting dragged closer to his pale, limp body. His bloodless lips neared, and he drew in a last feeble breath, drawing me in as well. Darkness surrounded me. I struggled, but there was no escape. When his breathing stopped, it felt like the door to a windowless room had slammed shut.

It was Saturday, November 15, but I didn't know that. I wouldn't understand the strange countdown of days that formed my existence until later. All I knew then was that I was alive, alone, and trapped in the body of a dead person.

Night

The first night was long—a gray, indefinite expanse of time. I couldn't see, hear, or feel anything. So I huddled, not moving, if a bodiless entity can be said to huddle. In my imagination at least, that's how I saw myself, my nonexistent arms wrapped around my nonexistent legs—a genie trapped in a jar for who knows how long.

There was no way to judge the passing of time. No change or differentiation between one moment and the next. No forwards or backwards. Just a vast gray nothingness. Until a scream broke in.

Friday,
November 14

The scream tore through the darkness, trailing a stream of sunlight. I tried following the light out, but something kept me anchored. Looking down, I saw Dan's body in bed. He slapped the alarm clock with a meaty hand, then scratched the stubble on his cheek. Both his wrists appeared fine now—not a scratch or bandage on them. There wasn't even a scar where the cuts had been. That surprised me. Although his skin had a pinkish hue to it and he was breathing, in my memory he remained dead as a squirrel squished on the road.

I fought to pull away, but I was trapped inside him. Then the alarm screeched again. Dan buried his head beneath his pillow. Brilliant. You'd think that when an alarm is blaring, the sensible thing would be to turn it off and go back to sleep. Instead, he kept pulling more blankets over his head. He even grabbed a sweatshirt off the floor and bundled it across his ears. The guy was like a tortoise trying to bury himself in dirty laundry. This went on for *way* too long, until someone pounded the wall and a voice I recognized as his sister's told him to "Wake the hell up!"

Dan fumbled blindly with the alarm's buttons for nearly a minute before dragging his head out from under his pillow and finding the switch. Then he sat up and rubbed his eyes. I hoped he would shower, because his hair reeked of stale smoke.

I sank into him, wondering why he smelled like the wrong side of a bonfire. The deeper I got, the more I could sense what he sensed. I heard his heart thumping inside his chest and felt the weight of his body on his bones. Beneath all those physical sensations, though, whispered something else. His thoughts, maybe? There were so many whispers braided together, it sounded like a river rushing over rocks. I drifted closer until the whispers swirled around me, tugging at me, but I couldn't discern what any one whisper said. There was just this general sense of his mood. He seemed irritated and sleepy.

I felt better keeping my distance from the whispers. With effort, I stretched my awareness far enough away so that I could almost perceive Dan from the outside. He slouched on the edge of a bed that was set against one wall of a mostly bare room. There was a desk, a dresser, and a few shelves with books and some dusty football trophies on them. Drifts of wrinkled clothes cluttered the floor. I tried to look at the few posters decorating the walls, but most of what I saw, heard, smelled, and felt continued to be directed by him—as if I were stuck in a car, and all I could do was move around a little and watch things go by while he drove. He stared at a calendar hanging on the wall beside his bed. The top part showed a photo of a gazelle jumping over a crocodile. Below this it said COURAGE: *the ability to do something stupid and run like hell.*

All the days on the calendar were blank, except for a cluster toward the end of the month that had been circled with *Thanksgiving break—visit Dad* scrawled across them. Dan reached for the calendar, and his whispering thoughts grew louder and more anxious. For a moment, I expected him to count the days until Thanksgiving break or turn the page to look at December, but then he seemed to come to a decision. He lowered his hand and turned away. The whispers gradually subsided as he shuffled down the hall toward the bathroom.

I cringed when he reached for the bathroom door. I didn't want to see the puddles of blood, dissolving pills, and sickly pink stains on the rug again. No matter how

I fought to get away from there, though, it made no difference. I couldn't leave, and I couldn't stop him from walking. I couldn't even close his eyes or make him look in a different direction.

Dan pushed open the bathroom door and flicked on a light, blinking at the stark floor tiles and bright-white tub.

The bathroom wasn't exactly clean, yet compared to the bloody mess I expected, it appeared immaculate. No blood stained the rug or tiles, and there were no pills on the floor. Even the shampoo bottles Dan had knocked over were back in place.

Dan slid off his boxers and stepped into the shower. The cold tub stung his feet, but the water soon warmed, pelting his back with hot drops. He moved mechanically, rubbing shampoo into his hair. A tangy-sweet scent of grapefruit and bubble gum filled his senses while warmth trickled down his spine. I focused on the physical sensations, marveling at how all the tiny hairs on his arm lined up as water streamed over his muscles and pooled around his toes. However I got here, it felt amazing to exist, but Dan seemed indifferent to it all. Dead to the world.

He shut off the water, toweled himself dry, and got out. Then he went about his morning business, oblivious to me riding around inside him. Without access to his thoughts, he seemed like a walking corpse. A zombie.

I watched Dan dry his hair, put gel in it, wet it again, then gel it again, until he finally gave up and doused himself with way too much cologne.

"You done plucking your nose hairs yet?" called a familiar voice through the door.

"Just a minute."

"Come on, Dan. You're taking forever. I need to get ready."

He ran his fingers through his hair one last time and opened the door.

The girl who'd discovered his bleeding body in the tub stood on the other side with her hands braced on her hips. She raised her chin and jutted out her bony elbows like a hedgehog trying to appear bigger.

"All yours," he said, avoiding her gaze.

Teagan sniffed. "It smells like a country club in here." She nodded at the bottle of cologne by the sink. "Have you been drinking that stuff again?"

I laughed, but Dan didn't. "Very funny," he grumbled.

Teagan crinkled her nose and stuck out her tongue. I was beginning to like her. In spite of her heavy black eyeliner, she appeared childish and nervous. I remembered how she'd come apart when she discovered her brother's suicide. Beneath her insults and tough posturing, I saw the opposite — a girl who cared so much it scared her.

Dan didn't appear to notice any of this, though. He blew past Teagan and shuffled into the kitchen to pour himself a bowl of cereal.

Watching him spill cereal on the counter and dribble milk down the side of the carton repulsed me. Then the crunching. Slurping. Swallowing. The zombie seemed barely conscious of what he did. He ate out of habit, shoveling soggy bites into his mouth.

His mom bustled about the kitchen, but Dan didn't say a word to her. She wore a starched white blouse and business slacks. Although a little on the heavy side, she was still fairly attractive, with pale-green eyes and dark hair cut in a stylish bob. She held a bagel in one hand and a sponge in the other, eating while she wiped up the mess that Dan had made on the countertop. Then she put away the cereal box and the milk he'd left out.

"Will you go to the grocery store after school?" she asked, brushing crumbs off the table in front of Dan.

He didn't respond.

"Are you listening?"

"Yeah," he said, sounding like she'd interrupted him in the middle of composing a symphony. "You want me to go today?"

"Yes, today," said his mom. "We don't have anything for dinner." She tossed the sponge into the sink and dug through her purse, pulling out a credit card. "Here. Just get what's on the list. Can you do that?"

"Yeah," repeated Dan. A caveman could have been more articulate.

"You have to make sure to get angel hair pasta, not the regular kind. And don't buy avocados if they're not ripe."

He took the card and set it on the counter.

His mom hesitated. Then she picked up the list and credit card and stuffed them into the front pocket of his backpack. "So you don't forget them," she said.

Teagan strolled into the kitchen a moment later and poured herself a cup of coffee. Their mom watched her — a mix of concern and disapproval playing across her face. "You need to eat something for breakfast," she said.

"That cereal tastes like dog food," replied Teagan.

"I thought you liked this cereal."

Teagan rolled her eyes and sipped her coffee.

"At least eat something healthy at school."

"Are maggots healthy?" asked Teagan. "Because that's what they serve. Tricia found a maggot in her rice."

Their mom checked her watch and cursed. "I'm late," she said, turning to Dan. "Think you can give your sister a ride today?"

"No."

"Excuse me?"

"I'm not taking Teagan," Dan said in a quiet monotone.

"Why not?" questioned their mom, looking from Dan to Teagan. "Last time I checked, you both went to the same school."

"He doesn't want me to embarrass him in front of his friends," Teagan said.

"That's right," Dan replied. "Stay away from my friends."

Teagan's jaw clenched. She tried to look angry, but from the way her shoulders dropped, I could tell that Dan's words had hurt her. I wanted to punch him for being such a jerk. "Some of your friends are nice to me, you know," she said.

"Like who?"

"Like Finn."

Dan glared at his sister. "Don't talk to Finn."

"You can't tell me who to talk to."

"I mean it, Teagan."

"Why—jealous? Afraid he'll like me more than you?"

Dan scowled. "He probably only talked to you to make fun of you."

Teagan slammed her coffee cup onto the counter. "You're such a prick," she spat, and stormed out of the room.

Their mom sighed. I sensed this wasn't the first time

fights like this had happened. "I don't understand why you can't be nicer to her," she said to Dan. "She looks up to you."

"She shouldn't," he said.

Their mom grabbed her purse. "Teagan, you ready? Get in the car. We're leaving."

On the way to school, I kept thinking about how cruel Dan had been to Teagan. *You really are a prick,* I said to him, but if he heard me, he didn't show it. He just ground his teeth and drove, barely looking at the buildings we passed or the leaves swirling along the sidewalk in the fall breeze.

After a few minutes, he pulled into the parking lot of a building that looked like a prison—brick walls the color of bread, slit-thin windows too narrow to crawl out of, and a complete lack of landscaping. Welcome to Jefferson High.

Dan turned off his car and stared at the front entrance, where his mom had probably dropped Teagan off just minutes before. In fact, Teagan was still there, standing near the flagpole to the left of the main doors, talking to a large girl in a billowy black skirt and black T-shirt. Dan didn't pay much attention to his sister, though. Instead, he focused on a cluster of students gathered around a bell hanging from a bright orange archway.

Most of the guys huddled by the bell wore varsity jackets and baseball caps. They laughed and punched each other's shoulders while a few girls lingered nearby. As I watched, it became clear that they all orbited around one guy in the center. He had straight hair swept casually across his brow and a lazy smile. Whenever he talked, everyone seemed to lean in and listen. I wondered what he said to captivate people's attention like that. Then the first bell sounded and students funneled inside.

The guy with the lazy smile caught Teagan's eye as she turned to enter. He said something to her and she smiled back, looking happier than I'd seen her all morning. Dan dug his fingers into his thighs, seeming upset by this, but I had the opposite reaction. *Good,* I thought. *At least someone's nice to her.*

School wasn't much fun. No one greeted Dan when he arrived, and a few people even snickered or whispered as he passed. The zombie shuffled on, ignoring them. Once he got to his first class, he tossed his backpack to the floor and slumped in the back row.

The second bell sounded and announcements were made. Then the teacher began class. After a few minutes, Dan nodded off. Asleep, he didn't do much to distract me, so I had time to question some of the things I'd seen that morning, starting with *Why isn't Dan dead?*

For that matter, what am I doing here? I wondered. *And who am I? And why can't I remember anything before waking up in the tub?*

More questions poured out, quick as water flowing through a crack in a dam, each one making the breach a little larger.

Am I supposed to be here? How long will this last?

The questions kept coming—a clamoring flood of unknowns. I had no answers to silence them. Nothing solid to cling to. It felt like my whole being might unravel and drown in uncertainty.

Am I crazy?

Dan snapped awake, perhaps sensing my panic.

He looked around, but no one seemed to be watching him. Then he rubbed the drool from the corners of his mouth and tapped his pen against his thumb. I focused on the sting of the plastic on his knuckle. The sharp, definitive sensation calmed me. It seemed to calm Dan as well. After a few minutes, he stopped tapping and dozed off again.

This time I narrowed my focus to one question. *Why am I here?* That seemed like a good place to start, because if I could figure out why I was here, then the answers to my other questions might fall into place.

I sorted through everything I remembered. The drops of blood turning the bathwater pink. Dan's body going limp. His sister and mom watching, distraught, while the paramedics wheeled him out. And then this morning he looked fine, like his death had never happened. Everything was back to normal. Only it wasn't normal, was it? Things felt off. Out of place. So maybe I was supposed to fix something. That could be the reason I was here.

Class ended and Dan shuffled to a different room. He didn't talk with anyone in the hall. For most of the morning, he just zoned out in various classrooms, giving me time to think. Who knows—maybe he was thinking, too.

Dan didn't perk up until lunch. His chest tightened and his palms grew sweaty as he approached the avocado-green cafeteria. Apparently, food made him nervous. Students crowding the long white tables chattered noisily, and the air smelled of grilled cheese and chicken soup. The zombie stared at a table near the front where several guys I recognized from outside the school sat.

Were these his friends? Outwardly, he looked similar to some of them with their muscular arms, tight polo shirts, and athletic builds. He even had a varsity jacket like them, although he'd left it in his locker. Then the guy with the lazy smile who'd been nice to Teagan noticed Dan and waved.

I wanted to sit with him, but Dan's gaze slid to another table across the room where Teagan sat. After a few seconds, I realized he wasn't looking at his sister but at a girl with dark purple hair sitting across from her. His stomach fluttered and his heart began to race. I grew anxious as well, only it was a good anxious.

Even from a distance, several things about the girl

stood out. There was her hair, of course, colored a vivid dark eggplant shade, and her clothes — forest-green shirt, purple skirt that matched her hair, and striped leggings. And there were her eyes, intense yet wistful. Other people at the table kept looking at her, but she avoided meeting anyone's gaze. Instead, she looked at her hands and the door and the wall, appearing slightly removed from the rest of the students, as if she were the only person rendered in color in a black-and-white world and she was slightly embarrassed by this fact. For a moment, I thought the zombie might actually sit with her. Then she stood, set her tray on the stack by the trash, and headed for the side doors.

I wanted to follow her. Luckily, Dan seemed intrigued by her as well. He hurried out the back doors of the cafeteria, arriving just in time to catch her turning down a hall.

Dan looked over his shoulder warily before heading after her. The hall she'd taken was lined with student drawings. WHO WE ARE: SELF-PORTRAIT ASSIGNMENT read a banner hanging across the entrance. The girl paused near the end. She reached up for one of the drawings, only it was hung too high. She could barely touch the bottom inch or so.

"Cat," Dan said.

The girl startled. Her eyes flicked to his and narrowed.

"What are you doing?" Dan asked.

"Taking this down," she said.

"Why?"

"Because I don't want people to see it anymore."

Dan looked at the drawing. Most of the portraits decorating the hall were distorted charcoal sketches. A few took more rigid approaches, capturing an accurate self-image. But the one Cat reached for blew them all away.

Instead of a close-up of her face, Cat had drawn several versions of herself sitting around a table, having a tea party. She was a girl in a fluffy dress, sipping her tea at the head of the table, and she was the figure next to her in a jaunty top hat, looking slightly deranged as she poured cream into an overflowing cup. A small mouse version of herself peeked out of a teapot in the middle of the table, appearing wet and sad, one mouse ear flopping over her eye. Last of all, she was in the foreground, depicted as a girl with bunny ears looking away from the viewer, the jaw-length cut of her hair clearly matching Cat's own. Hovering above the scene, like a horizontal crescent moon, floated a bright disembodied grin.

While everyone else had drawn shallow surface images, Cat had portrayed something far deeper. Fragments of herself, hidden in herself. A sudden, inexplicable sense of connection came over me.

Dan checked the hall before he spoke. "Did the cops catch you last night?" he asked.

"No." Cat stopped peeling her portrait off the wall and looked down.

He studied her. A few freckles dotted her nose, and a diagonal scar ran like a small lightning bolt through the crease above her mouth. The thin, jagged scar made her top lip the tiniest bit crooked. I found this one imperfection to be unexpectedly beautiful. *She* was beautiful, although she didn't appear to know it. Instead, she seemed self-conscious. Perhaps she thought Dan was staring at her scar in a negative way, yet that wasn't how I saw it at all.

For me, the scar was one more sign of how different she was. And how brave. I wondered if every smile for her required a small act of defiance—a refusal to succumb to the scar that she thought marred her face. And I wanted to kiss her then. To kiss that perfect scar above her lip.

"Sorry about the house," Dan said, jarring me out of my thoughts. He sounded nervous. Maybe he'd been distracted by thoughts of kissing her, too. After all, he *had* been staring at her lips. "If the cops question you, you can blame everything on me. I don't care. I'll tell them it was an accident."

"Like it was an accident that you were there?" replied Cat.

"I was trying to help you."

"I don't need your help. You think you know me, Dan, but you don't."

That's not true, I whispered. I wanted to tell her that I knew her the way a bird knows the wind. The way a fish knows the river. The way a leaf turns to the sun no matter where it is in the sky. But only Dan got to speak.

"That's not true," he muttered.

Cat shook her head. "I can't talk to you anymore."

"Because of what happened at the house?"

"Because of everything."

"Cat, it's not what you think—"

"How do you know what I think?" she interrupted. "I remember more now. About what happened. What *you* did. Am I just a game to you? A broken trophy to add to your shelf?"

"What?" Dan hesitated. "No," he said, but his whispers increased, taking on guilty tones. *Had* she been a game to him?

Anger gripped me. Somehow he'd hurt her, and now he was making it worse. Hurting her more.

Cat must have caught Dan's hesitation as well. "Tell me this," she challenged. "Why now? Why did you suddenly become interested in me now?"

"I've always been interested in you."

"Bullshit."

"It's true," he said. "Do you remember in sixth grade, after my dad left and your mom left, those sessions we had to go to? You were the only one who really got it. The

26

only one who understood what I was going through. I've never been able to talk with anyone like that."

"Then why did you stop talking to me? For years, you barely said a word to me."

"I know. I'm sorry. It's just—"

"I know why," she said. "You don't have to lie about it. It must have been hard being so popular." She bit her lip. It occurred to me that none of the versions of herself she'd drawn had her scar. In her portrait, she'd erased that part of herself.

"I can't believe how naive I was," she continued. "When you asked me to the party, I thought you might actually like me."

"I do," he said.

"You sure have a funny way of showing it."

"Look, about what happened . . . I know it's my fault."

"That's a stupid thing to say."

"But it's true," Dan said. "I'm sorry."

"You're *sorry*?" A hurt laugh escaped Cat. "Is that supposed to make it better? I should smile now and forget it?"

"No."

"Good. Because I can't forget it. I won't." She drew a shaky breath. "Don't you get it, Dan? I don't want to see you ever again."

"Cat—" The zombie reached for her.

"*Don't touch me,*" she said. "I mean it. Don't be nice to

me. Don't give me things. Don't even look at me. If you care about me at all, you'll leave me the fuck alone."

She glared at Dan, her intense gaze burning into him. Then her eyes softened slightly around the edges. My hopes surged. Irrational as it might seem, I felt she could see me, trapped within him. Why else would she stare at him like that after telling him to leave her alone? The zombie's pulse sped up. It was dizzying. Then Cat seemed to remember herself, and her anger at Dan.

She turned and yanked down her portrait. The corners ripped but she didn't stop. She crumpled up the drawing and retreated down the hall.

I wanted to call to her and tell her I understood—not simply the things she said, but the things she couldn't say. I would have given anything to be able to talk, but she kept going, disappearing around the corner. And the zombie didn't move.

For the rest of the day, I couldn't stop thinking about Cat. Whenever Dan changed classes, I clung to the hope that I'd see her again. I think he was looking for her, too. When his last class ended, he checked the hallways where the lockers were and circled the school a couple times, but there was no sign of her. He finally shuffled across the empty parking lot and drove home.

He didn't do much after that—just watched some TV until Teagan returned. Then he hid in his bedroom and searched the Internet, but I didn't pay attention to him. I kept imagining what I'd say to Cat if I could talk to her. How I'd chisel through the walls that kept us apart.

Eventually, the zombie flopped on his bed and stared at the wall. Just as he'd done that morning, he stretched his hand toward the calendar, only this time, he lifted the bottom pages. Two words had been etched into the drywall. No wonder he'd hung the calendar there. If his mom saw what he'd done, she'd freak. He dragged his fingers across the words, feeling the rough grooves and cuts that formed them. It wasn't until he pulled his hand back that I was able to read what they said:

SAVE HER

A shiver coursed through me. Or maybe it went through Dan and I was sensing his reaction. Still, I couldn't shake the feeling that the message was meant for me.

The garage door pulled Dan out of his daze. He pressed the calendar back so it covered the words and listened to the sounds of his mom hanging up her coat. Her footsteps grew louder, stopping outside his door.

"Dan, where are the groceries?" she asked.

"I didn't have time to get them," Dan shouted back.

"I asked you to do one thing."

"It's no big deal. I'll go now."

His mom groaned. "It's too late . . ." Her voice receded, muttering to no one about how she was tired of having to handle everything on her own.

I felt bad for her. She didn't seem mean, just overwhelmed. The words beneath the calendar came back to me. SAVE HER. Except who did the "her" refer to? His mom? Teagan? Cat? And how was he supposed to save them? He couldn't even get the groceries.

Dan paced his room and glanced at the calendar again. Then he pulled out his cell phone, scrolled through the names to DAD, and hit CALL.

"Danny?" answered a man's voice.

"Hi, Dad."

"Listen, I can't talk right now. We're sitting down for dinner."

"Okay," said Dan.

There was an awkward pause.

"So is everything all right?" the voice on the other end asked.

"Yeah. I just . . . wanted to see how the weather is there," said Dan. "See what I should pack."

"It's pretty much always the same here."

"Sunny and seventy?"

"Blue skies every day," replied his dad.

"Nice," said Dan. "I can't wait to go outside and have some guy time."

Dan's dad didn't respond right away. In the background, I heard two young children calling for attention. I pictured him fending off chipper, well-adjusted kids. "Well," he started, returning to the phone, "it won't just be us guys. Marcy and the girls will be here, too."

"I know. But maybe we can go out alone sometime. Get away from things."

"On *Thanksgiving*?" replied his dad.

"Maybe another day?"

"We'll see." His dad sounded tired. "Keep in mind I have to work, okay? I don't get all those days off like you do. Speaking of which, I heard you got suspended."

"Who told you that?"

"Your mom mentioned it."

"Oh."

"Is that why you're not at football right now?" asked his dad. "They keeping you benched for a week?"

"No. I quit football."

"What do you mean you quit?" The phone crackled and the kids' voices faded. I pictured Dan's dad retreating to another room. "You're starting receiver," he continued in a terse, staccato voice. "You can't quit."

"It's just a game," said Dan.

"No, it's not. Colleges really look at this stuff."

"I wasn't good enough for college ball."

"That's not the point," said his dad. "It's about being well-rounded. Showing character. Your team depends on you, Dan."

Dan didn't say anything for several seconds.

His dad groaned. "Here's what you need to do. Call your coach. Tell him you changed your mind. Beg him to let you back."

"I can't," said Dan.

"Why not?"

"Because I don't want to be on the team anymore."

"Dammit, Dan. If you blow this, you won't get a second chance. It will haunt you for the rest of your life. Understand?"

Dan slumped on his bed. "Yeah."

"You're smart enough to know better. Stuff like this goes on your transcript. It stays with you. Financial aid is very competitive. Even little things can mean the difference between being accepted into a good college and being rejected."

"I know."

"You can't afford to mess up."

"I know."

"You're better than this."

Silence.

"So will you call your coach?"

"I guess."

"Good," said his dad. A kid's high-pitched squeal in the background turned to crying. "I should get going."

"Okay." Another long pause. "Hey, Dad?"

"Yeah?" The hollow reply sounded just like Dan's own. No mystery where the zombie had gotten his gift for communication from. The kid's cries grew louder.

"Nothing," said Dan. "I just wanted to say good-bye."

"Bye, Danny."

Dan ended the call and stared at his computer. I could hear his mom leaving for the grocery store. A few minutes later, Dan snuck into the garage. He pulled a dusty toolbox off the shelf and rifled through a mess of screwdrivers, scissors, and other tools until he found a yellow package of single-edge razor blades—like the ones I'd seen in the bathroom after he slit his wrists.

All at once, things started to make sense. The events I remembered and the events from today began to shift and fall into place. It wasn't that Dan's death hadn't happened. It was that it hadn't happened *yet*.

Dan pocketed the blades and turned to his car—an old two-door coupe that was supposed to look sporty but with its faded paint job and rusty wheel wells just looked sad. He started the engine. The garage door was closed, which made me think he might asphyxiate himself. Part of me hoped he would, so I could be free of this whole mess. But after a couple minutes, Dan turned off the car and pulled out the keys. He pried them off the key chain. They were the same two beat-up keys I'd seen on the sticky note with FOR TEAGAN written on it.

Dan popped open the hood of the car. He stared at the engine for several seconds, then did what he could—checked the fluids, dug out a dirty funnel from a box on the shelf and added a quart of oil, touched a few belts, and wiped some grime off the battery with a rag. Satisfied, he let the hood fall shut.

In that moment, I almost liked him. I think he wanted to do something good, and in his mixed-up mind, I suppose leaving his sister his car was that. Granted, she'd probably never drive the damn thing. She'd probably even hate looking at it and remembering that he'd given it to her, because now I knew, with complete certainty, that tomorrow—my yesterday—Dan would kill himself.

Night

When night closed around me again, I didn't want to be stuck in the zombie a moment longer. Since his eyes were shut and he seemed unconscious, I couldn't sense much physically — there was just the gray, indefinite expanse I'd been stuck in before. But I refused to let that stop me. I walked into the darkness, picturing myself getting farther from Dan. Each time I got ten or so steps away, something tugged me back. It felt like a million rubber bands were tied to my being, and the farther I stretched from Dan, the harder they pulled. I tried again, only this time, when I reached my limit, I summoned all my will and threw myself into the abyss.

Something ripped. It felt horrible—like tearing out every hair on my body all at once. Then I tumbled into moonlight.

Looking down, I saw the zombie turn in his sleep. I quickly backed up so I wouldn't get drawn into him again. Before I knew it, I was running across the front yard.

Once I crossed the street, I slowed. No alarms went off. Nothing tugged me to Dan. No one even seemed to have noticed that I'd gone. I was free!

A whoop of joy nearly escaped my lips, but I swallowed it down. No sense in pushing my luck.

I checked my surroundings. The street looked empty, and most of the houses appeared dark. A silver half-moon illuminated the crisp fall sky. From what I'd observed of the town earlier, when I'd been trapped in Dan, it wasn't very large. I tried to get my bearings. Several of the trees lining the street had either changed color or lost their leaves already. I followed the sidewalk toward where the glow of streetlights over the rooftops appeared brightest. After a couple blocks, I turned onto a wider street. A car waited at the intersection, but other than that, there wasn't any traffic.

I headed toward a cluster of two-story brick buildings that looked like the main drag. A drugstore, a clothing store, and a couple of bars lined the street. Two women staggered out of one bar, followed by a large man. They ambled to a pickup truck.

"Excuse me," I called, but they didn't look at me.

I raised my hand—partly to signal to them and partly to prove to myself that I was there. My fingers were slightly smaller than Dan's, and my nails seemed better taken care of than his, but I appeared every bit as real as him. And I certainly felt real. I took a deep breath and tried again.

"Hey! Over here!" I shouted.

Still no response.

"Hey, butt face!"

Nothing. Not even a scowl.

Frantically, I searched for someone else. A couple guys in their early twenties lingered in front of the bar across the street, smoking cigarettes. I jumped in front of them, but they kept talking as if nothing had happened.

My stomach sank. Perhaps I should have expected this. When I'd floated above Dan my first day here, no one had seen me. Still, I couldn't help feeling disappointed. I'd thought that if I escaped the zombie, I'd be just like everyone else. I'd get to live my life. But this was almost worse than being stuck in Dan. At least during the day, people saw him and reacted. Now I felt utterly invisible.

"Sucks, doesn't it?" someone said. I zeroed in on the voice, discerning a large, round-shouldered guy standing by a lamppost. He appeared hazy at first, but the more I looked at him, the clearer he became.

"Damn, man! You heard me!" he said. "I thought you might. You're not like them." He pointed to the guys smoking in front of the bar. They looked heavy and rigid compared to him, as if they were sculpted out of brass. "You're like me, aren't you?" he continued. "A rider."

I glanced over my shoulder to see if he might be talking to someone else. But there was no one else. "A *rider?*"

"Dude, this is sweet! How long have you been here?"

"Not long. I . . . just arrived."

"Yesterday or today?" he pressed.

"I'm not sure."

The guy leaned closer. He had a soft, slightly pudgy face. *"Or tomorrow?"* he added, lowering his voice. "Did you get here tomorrow?"

The two guys who'd been smoking stubbed out their cigarettes and went back into the bar.

"Are you moving backwards?" continued the guy. "Riding the corpse in reverse?"

What he was saying sounded crazy, even to me. It also sounded right. I looked around, checking to see if anyone else might be listening in. Then I nodded.

"Yes!" He pumped his fist. "I knew it. For three days, I've been freaking out, but I knew I wasn't tripping. Weird, isn't it?"

"I guess."

"This is cool. You're lucky I found you."

"I am?"

"Yeah, dude. I can show you things. Besides, it sucks being alone." He veered into the street. "I mean, watching chicks undress is fun," he said. "But after a while, it's like that joke about the guy who gets shipwrecked on a tropical island with a supermodel."

I had no clue what he was talking about. "A supermodel?"

The guy didn't slow down. Apparently, not speaking to anyone in three days left him eager to get some words in. "So they're shipwrecked there," he continued, "and at first it's rough, but after a few months they get to know each other, and they have this perfect life together, eating coconuts and living in a bamboo shack. Until one day this suitcase washes ashore, and it's full of some dude's clothes. So the guy asks the supermodel to put them on. He tells her it's the one thing he really wants. She thinks it's kind of kinky, dressing up in some dude's clothes like this, but she does it. And once she's all dressed up in the shirt and pants and baseball cap, with her hair tucked under the cap and everything, the guy turns to her and says, 'Dude! You'll never guess who I've been sleeping with.'" The guy looked at me and laughed—a high, giggling sound like a chipmunk. "Get it?"

The thought that he might be insane crossed my mind.

He paused in the middle of the road. "Hey, look! A quarter!" he said, stooping to pick up the coin.

"There's a truck coming," I warned.

"It's like stuck here," he said, refusing to leave the coin. The truck rushed closer, not even slowing down.

"Watch out!" I yelled.

Too late. The truck smacked into him and kept going, leaving him flat on the road.

I rushed over to the guy's body. His tongue lolled out the side of his mouth, and his arms and legs splayed out at odd angles. He wasn't moving. "Shit!" I said, not knowing what to do. I didn't even know the guy's name. "Shit, shit, shit . . ."

"Dude!" he said, sitting up. "You *are* a newbie!"

I jumped.

"Man, you should see your face."

"The truck—" I stammered. Had I hallucinated the whole thing?

"You thought I was road jerky, didn't you?" he said, grinning.

I felt sick.

"Sorry, dude. Just messing with you. They go right through us. Everything goes through us," he added. "It doesn't even tickle. Sure is a rush, though."

"Yeah," I muttered, leaving the road. "Some rush."

"I'm TR," said the guy, falling in step beside me. "It's short for Terc's rider, because that's the name of the corpse I'm stuck in. Terc. Or Tercio. So the next time I get flattened by a semi, you can call me TR instead of 'Shit.'" He laughed. "I totally got you, man."

Although I wanted to curse him out, there was something harmless and good-natured about the guy that made him hard to stay angry at. "I need a cup of coffee," I said.

"Sure." TR started down the block to a brightly lit diner. "I'll buy."

On the way, TR told me about how he woke up. His first memory was of his corpse getting his head cracked open on a steering wheel. "It was like an egg," he said. "I mean, his head was seriously cracked with stuff leaking out." He looked at me and shrugged like it was no big deal, but I could tell it bothered him.

TR continued talking, not waiting for a response. He described his first night, which sounded pretty similar to mine—a gray, indefinable emptiness. Then, when he woke, he was stuck in the corpse, only the guy's head was back together again. "Like Humpty Dumpty," he said, "except not, because no one could put Humpty Dumpty together again."

It took TR three whole days of riding around in Terc before he figured out that he was going backwards. From what I gathered, it hadn't been easy to spend all that time alone. Despite his jokes and laughter, I think he felt just as lost as I did.

"I call him Waster," said TR, referring to his corpse. "The guy is seriously wasted all the time. It's no wonder he got scrambled." He smiled at his joke. "Man, I'm glad I found you. I was bored off my flipping rocker. So what about you? What's your corpse like?"

"He's a zombie," I replied.

"A zombie!" TR bellowed. "That's good!"

We stopped at a diner with a neon-pink sign above the entrance: THE COFFEE SPOT. I tried to open the door, but I couldn't grab the handle. My fingers passed through it three times while TR watched.

"You're one funny dude," he said. Then he walked straight through the glass into the bright interior.

I debated following him, only the thought of intentionally stepping through glass made my skin crawl. I decided to wait for someone else to open the door so I could slip in. After a couple of minutes, though, I began to worry that TR might wander off. Already things felt a little too quiet without him. Tentatively, I pushed my hand through the glass. Then I closed my eyes and stepped forward. TR was right—it didn't hurt, but that didn't mean it felt okay.

I spotted TR messing around behind the counter. "About time," he said. "Watch this." He leaned his head into a pot of coffee. "Argh! It burns!" he yelled, barely able to keep from laughing. Next he put his hands in the fryer. "I'm bacon!"

It freaked me out to watch him, which was probably why he kept doing stuff. I scanned the diner for a place to sit.

"Get it, man?" TR called. "I'm *bakin'*."

The diner wasn't very big. A few middle-aged guys sporting flannel shirts occupied the counter, while students chugging coffee and cramming for tests took up several booths. A waitress nearly shoved a pie cart into me. I stepped aside, but she didn't so much as glance in my direction.

"Takes some getting used to," said TR. "It's like they're not even there, isn't it?"

"Or we aren't," I said.

"Speak for yourself," he answered. "Anyhow, no point waiting to be seated." He walked through the counter toward a booth near the back.

I dodged the waitress and hurried after him. Several

high-school students had taken over the back section of the diner. I recognized a few. In one booth sat the heavy-set girl, dressed all in black, who'd been standing next to Teagan before school. Next to her slouched a skinny punk guy with facial piercings. And across from them sat Cat. Her back was to me, but there was no mistaking her purple hair and slender neck.

"What's up?" asked TR.

"I know her," I said, pointing to Cat.

"*You* know her?" asked TR.

"I mean the zombie knows her."

He nodded and strode over to Cat's booth to get a better look. "She's cute—if you like weird chicks," he said. "I'm more into fake blondes with a lot of love, if you know what I mean."

I drifted closer to her table. Cat poured powdered cream into her coffee, letting it form a tiny white island that gradually sank into the brown liquid. The skinny punk guy and the girl in black talked about what they might do that night.

"*Hi,*" I said. If anyone could hear me, it would be Cat.

Her head tilted slightly, and she tucked her hair back behind her ear. Maybe it was wishful thinking, but I felt like she wanted to look at me, only she didn't know where to find me.

"*Hi,*" I repeated.

44

"Dude, give it up," said TR. "They're clueless." He clambered onto the divider between booths and hunched over their table like a gargoyle. "It's like watching TV. Talk to it all you want, but it won't answer."

"I know," I said, yet deep down I didn't believe TR. There had to be some part of Cat that heard me. Some part that could sense my intentions. But with TR sitting there, I wasn't about to try talking to her again.

I perched on the back of the booth across from him and watched her pour more powdered cream into her coffee. It formed another tiny white island that floated for a moment before dissolving around the edges and sinking.

The skinny punk guy was talking about going to some abandoned house. "We could sneak back there and drink some wine," he said. "Then paint the walls more."

The girl in black stayed silent. I think they were both waiting for Cat to respond.

Cat set down the powdered-cream container. "No. We can't," she said without looking up.

"Why not?"

Cat watched the last bit of powdered cream dissolve into her coffee. "Because my island keeps sinking."

The girl in black and the skinny guy shared a concerned look.

"You okay?" asked the girl in black.

"Sure," said Cat. "Sink your island and start over, right?"

"If your island sinks, where do you start over?" asked the skinny guy.

"Good point."

"Not to mix metaphors, but maybe you should just drink the coffee," said the girl in black.

Cat poured more powdered cream into her coffee, forming another doomed temporary island. "It's no use. Everything sinks."

"Told you this chick is weird," interjected TR.

I didn't argue with him. Still, out of all the people I'd seen, Cat made more sense to me than anyone. The sinking island, for instance, seemed like the perfect metaphor for all the questions I'd been drowning in and my desperate need to find solid ground to stand on. Every time I thought I knew something, though, more questions came up and eroded the edges, pulling me down again. So maybe it was the same for her. Something had happened and now she didn't know who she was anymore.

TR's attention shifted to a waitress refilling coffee at a nearby table. She leaned over, giving him a view of her cleavage. "Now, that's what I'm talking about." He nodded to the waitress.

I focused on Cat and her friends, wanting to learn everything I could about her.

"It's Friday," continued the skinny guy. "We have to do something fun."

Cat pushed her coffee cup back. "Count me out," she said. "I've had all the fun I can handle."

The girl in black pulled a cigarette out of her purse. She tapped it on the table, packing the tobacco. "We can split it on the way home."

Cat nodded and stood. Instinctively, I stood with her.

"You going to follow them?" asked TR.

"Maybe," I said, not wanting to seem too eager.

"Cool. I'll join you."

"You sure?"

"It's not like I've got someplace better to be," he answered.

We stayed a few feet behind Cat and the others as they exited into the parking lot. I learned that the girl in black's name was Tricia, and they called the skinny guy Spooner. The three of them cut through the lot behind the Coffee Spot to a residential neighborhood.

"At first, all I did was follow people," TR said. "I even tried to pretend I was part of people's conversations, adding comments when they spoke, but no one heard me. It was pitiful, dude. Then I discovered that I could walk through walls." He gave me a wry grin and raised his eyebrows. "I've seen all sorts of chicks naked, dude. Pretty girls. Naughty girls. Religious girls. Big girls. Older girls.

You name it. But even that got dull after a while. Or maybe not," he mused, looking at Cat.

"That's not why I'm following her," I said.

"Sure it isn't." TR drifted into the street. He shouted and jumped every time a car passed through him, like he was jumping ocean waves. "You should try this," he called after a few minutes.

Eventually, Cat and her friends arrived at an apartment complex. The place looked fairly run-down, with streaks on the cinder blocks from where air conditioners had dripped rusty water, brown paint flaking off window frames, and faded plastic kids' toys cluttering the courtyard. Cat said good-bye to the others and entered an apartment on the first floor while Tricia headed upstairs and Spooner skateboarded on.

I stayed outside and watched the lights in Cat's apartment flick on—first the living room, then her bedroom. At least I thought it was her bedroom, because the curtains covering the window were dark purple and green, which seemed like colors she'd pick.

"Now things get interesting," TR said.

"You better not—" I started, but he kept going. With an exaggerated step, he passed through the bricks.

I stood, staring at the wall.

TR's round head popped out a moment later, floating

48

above the bushes like a grinning jack-o'-lantern. "You gotta see this," he said, and ducked back in.

I wasn't about to let him add Cat to the list of girls he'd watched undress. Closing my eyes, I stepped forward.

Nothing felt different, but when I opened my eyes, the night sky had been replaced by purple walls and white Christmas lights. The sudden change disoriented me. Even the ceiling was purple, except for some green glow-in-the-dark stars scattered across it. Flamingos, crying turtles, and blue caterpillars inhabited shelves, and a flock of giant playing cards dangled from fishing line above the bed. A cat grinned on one wall among a field of painted mushrooms, while a collection of teapots covered the dresser. Compared to Dan's mostly bare walls, her room was a work of art.

Cat's voice drifted in from the hallway. She entered a moment later, speaking into her phone. When she closed the door behind her, I noticed another, smaller door painted on the inside with the words DRINK ME written above it.

"Good night, Dad," she said into the phone before hanging up. Then she shrugged off her backpack and jacket. She didn't glance at TR or me, but I still stepped back to stay out of her way. TR went around her room, studying all the figurines, teapots, and books on her shelves like they were objects in a museum.

After kicking off her boots, Cat flopped on the bed. According to the giant pocket watch–shaped clock on her bedside table, it was nearly midnight. Rather than going to sleep, Cat grabbed an iPod off her desk, pushed in the earbuds, and turned the volume up so loud I could hear it. Then she slid a shoe box out from under her bed. Inside, nestled in tissue paper, lay three figurines — a grinning cat, a white rabbit with a pocket watch, and a stumpy little man wearing a huge hat. The figurines didn't look all that special, but she stared at them for a long time, so they must have been important.

It surprised me when she dumped all three figurines into the trash. From the look on her face, I got the sense that she was throwing away more than just the figurines. Then she slumped back onto her bed and unzipped her sweatshirt.

"Let's go," I said to TR.

"Hold on. She's about to take off her shirt."

"That's why we're going."

"Damn, man — we waited forever for this."

"We're going," I repeated.

TR sighed. "Your loss, man," he said, and stepped through the wall.

I took one last look at Cat and followed him out.

TR wanted to find a train to stand in front of. I went with him, but I wasn't in much of a mood to get run over—even if the train would pass through me. After waiting on a trestle above a river for an hour, we walked to a nearby apartment building. Most of the lights were off and barely anyone seemed awake, but the stairs on the outside gave us something to climb. TR took the fire escape to the roof. He tried to get me to jump, but I had no desire to fall. Eventually, TR took the plunge alone. His large, plump body drifted back and forth like a falling leaf.

He jumped a few more times. The horizon slowly lightened, and birds chirped from rooftops. "We better head back," he said, studying the sky. "You don't want to be out when your corpse wakes up."

"Why not?"

"Trust me, you just don't want to be out." He set off toward Main Street.

The zombie's neighborhood was on the way, but I didn't want to go there. The thought of spending another day trapped in Dan repulsed me. "Hey," I said as we neared Dan's block, "do you know who we are?"

"What do you mean?"

"I mean, do you know why we're here? Stuck in the corpses?"

"Beats the hell out of me," TR replied. "Does anyone know why they're here?"

He had a point, although it didn't make me feel any better. I stopped in front of Dan's house. "This is where the zombie lives," I told him.

TR surveyed the place. "Lucky you."

I shrugged, but I wasn't ready to go in. "What if we're ghosts?"

"Hell, no." TR nodded toward Dan's house. *"They're the dead ones."*

"You're right."

"Maybe we're aliens," he continued. "Or angels. Or demons. Or mistakes. Who cares? It's like worrying about where you were before you were born or what happens after you die. You can't know the answers, so there's no use stressing over it."

"I guess," I said, although I didn't entirely agree.

"Like that joke," he continued. "You know — the one about the guy who staggers into an Alcoholics Anonymous meeting and says, 'Please, help, I've been in a terrible accident!' But nobody at the meeting moves. Finally, one of the dudes raises his hand and says, 'I was in an accident once.'"

"I don't get it."

"That's the point," TR said. "Sometimes thinking about it doesn't do any good. You just got to roll with it, you know?" He looked at Dan's house, then back at me. "So I'll meet you here tomorrow or yesterday or whatever?"

"Sure."

I waited until TR rounded the corner before heading back to the apartment complex where Cat lived.

She turned restlessly in bed. Tears streaked her face, as if she'd cried herself to sleep — her island still sinking.

One of her arms lay outside the covers. I stroked my fingers across her wrist, so delicately I could have been touching her. Gradually, her breathing calmed. Then I drifted around her room and looked at the things on her shelves and the figurines she'd thrown away. They lay in the garbage on top of some ripped-up paper. In the faint morning light, I could make out pieces of the self-portrait I'd watched her tear off the wall earlier.

I reached into the garbage, wishing I could smooth out these torn fragments of her and tape them all back together. But my fingers passed through the crumpled edges.

I thought of the message etched into Dan's wall. SAVE HER.

TR may have believed wondering why we were here was useless, but it wasn't. There had to be a purpose to my existence — a reason I'd been pulled backwards through the days, and Cat seemed part of it. Why else would I feel such a connection to her? Perhaps I *was* an angel, brought here to help her. Or save her. I may not have been able to physically save her, but there had to be something I could do — some way to make things better for her. And Teagan and Dan's mom for that matter. Some way to fix everything Dan had messed up.

For a while, I stayed by Cat's side, brushing my hands through her hair and whispering to her. I knew she couldn't consciously hear me, but maybe she'd sense me there and be comforted. "You're not alone," I told her. "I'm with you. I won't leave you."

Sunlight leaked through her curtains. I watched the bright line creep up her blanket. Soon Cat would get up for school, and I'd go with her and whisper good things to her and keep her safe.

At least, that's what I'd planned. Then a million tiny fishhooks lodged into my being and ripped me out of her room. Everything rushed past, merging into a long gray tunnel.

My head reeled. I thought I'd puke — which, for someone without a physical existence, is rather disturbing.

I slammed into the zombie right as he sat up and slapped his alarm clock silent.

The date on the clock read 11/13.

Welcome to yesterday.

Thursday, November 13

The zombie spent a good ten minutes staring at the floor before shuffling to the bathroom. Every aspect of my being prickled from being reeled back into him. I focused on his morning routine, hoping that might make me feel better. He did most things the same as the other day, except this morning a small scab marked his forehead. Bits of it washed off in the shower, although some bruising and a red patch remained, indicating where the wound had been. It looked like he'd jumped into a ceiling fan, or maybe someone had smacked him with a shovel. Whatever had happened, it didn't help — the zombie remained as clueless and infuriating as ever.

I don't know why Dan bothered me so much. Other people might be inconsiderate and self-absorbed, but they hadn't killed themselves. My first memory was of him throwing away the most precious thing, letting his life literally go down the drain. It was hard not to let that memory color everything else he did. I didn't think I'd ever be able to forgive him for hurting his mom and Teagan like he had, or for whatever he'd done to Cat.

But it was little things, too. I couldn't stand the way he mumbled his words and swallowed his food without tasting it. And I couldn't stand how he scuffed his heels as he walked, oblivious to how lucky he was to simply be able to move and talk and feel the ground beneath his feet. There was so much he ignored. This morning, for instance, his mom greeted him when he shuffled into the kitchen, but he didn't even grunt in response. Then he grabbed the orange-juice container in front of Teagan without offering her the smallest *good morning* or *hello.*

"You better hurry or you'll be late," said his mom as Dan poured himself some juice. "And don't leave the juice out. It'll spoil."

Dan set the orange-juice carton beside the refrigerator and took a sip from his glass.

"Are you listening?" asked his mom.

"Yeah," he mumbled.

She gave an exasperated sigh and put the orange juice

back in the refrigerator. "You're just like your father," she said. "Can you at least give your sister a ride? She needs to be there early for some—"

"History project," finished Teagan. "And I can't ride with him."

"Why not?" asked their mom.

"Because I need to go now," said Teagan. From the way she fiddled with her shirt, I could tell this wasn't her only reason. "I don't want to be late."

Their mom looked from Teagan to Dan, but the zombie merely shrugged. "I haven't eaten breakfast yet."

Their mom sighed again and checked her phone. "I'll drop you off, even though it's not on my way."

"If I had a car, you wouldn't have to take me," said Teagan. "I could take myself."

"You can't drive."

"Not yet, but I could take driver's ed this fall. I'm old enough."

"That costs money."

"It's not that expensive. And then I wouldn't be a burden to you."

"You're not a burden." Their mom grabbed her purse and paused before a hall mirror to primp her hair. "I just don't see why you can't go with your brother."

Teagan gave Dan a long look, waiting for him to say something. The zombie stared at his empty cereal bowl as if the fate of the world rested on what he put in it. I wanted to kick the dolt. He wasn't blind. He had to know that his sister wanted his attention.

"Get your things," said their mom. "We should have left five minutes ago."

Teagan grabbed her backpack and hurried out, while the zombie poured cornflakes into his bowl.

I perked up as soon as we got to school, hoping to run into Cat. Given how depressed she'd been the other night, I figured something bad must have happened recently. Otherwise, why would Tricia and Spooner act so concerned about her at the Coffee Spot? And why would she be angry at Dan? But knowing her past was like knowing my future. I couldn't be certain what had happened until it happened.

Essentially, I viewed life from the opposite direction as everyone else. My future was their past and their past my future, so while others perceived events in light of what *had* happened, I perceived them in light of what *would* happen. In English class, for instance, I knew exactly which vocabulary words Mr. Shepherd would include on the pop quiz the next day. And I knew which teacher would collect homework, and which student would be called on and confess he hadn't done the reading, and who would get a breakup text from her boyfriend. Out of all the countless details in a day, I knew exactly which ones would have a consequence tomorrow. It was like reading the end of a mystery before the beginning, so the clues were all obvious. Yet it was the *how* and *why* of it all that eluded me.

I worked on paying close attention to everything the zombie observed so I could trace effects back to causes. After the other day, I had a pretty good idea where Cat would be at lunch. Sure enough, she sat at the same table today that she would tomorrow. Tricia sat across from her, and Teagan slumped a few seats down.

Cat's gaze crossed Dan's, lingering a few seconds longer than seemed necessary. That snapped the zombie out of his trance. Then he did a curious thing—he glanced nervously at the table of guys wearing varsity jackets. It all happened in an instant, but it made me wonder what he might be worried about.

Dan retreated to the hallway to eat his lunch while pretending to do homework. In actuality, he drew spirals in the margins and scratched his head. No wonder he'd bomb the math quiz tomorrow. I wanted to go back and see Cat again, except the zombie wouldn't budge. When the period ended, he shuffled to biology, arriving before everyone else and sitting in the back corner.

Students filed in, occupying the seats around him. To

my surprise, Cat entered and sat in the third row. We actually had a class together! She must have ditched the other day after yelling at Dan.

Mr. Huber, the teacher, announced that they were going to start their dissections today. He rolled out a cart of dead frogs pinned to black wax-filled trays, one for each lab group. A sharp, vaguely chemical scent accompanied the frogs. "Brings back memories, doesn't it?" said Mr. Huber, sniffing loudly. Most of the students crinkled their noses at the smell, but I found it pleasantly familiar. The classroom had been rife with this scent the other day. "Of all the senses, smell is the one most closely associated with memory," said Mr. Huber.

Seeing the frogs whole was like witnessing a miracle. They appeared perfectly stitched together and healed after the massacre of splayed bodies and amputated organs I'd observed in class before. If I kept going backwards, the frogs would return to life, although I doubted I'd get to see it. They'd probably arrived at the school already pickled. Still, travel backwards long enough, and all wounds heal.

Three other people sat at Dan's lab table, but Dan didn't talk to any of them. After a few groans and jokes, they set to work cutting open the frog and identifying organs while filling out their lab reports. Dan stayed off to the side, stealing glances at Cat.

"Liver," said Ed, one of Dan's lab partners.

The zombie shifted his gaze back to his group. "Huh?"

"Number five. It's the liver, not the pancreas."

"Oh, right. Thanks."

"You okay, Dan?" asked Ed.

"Yeah," he said. His cheeks strained as he forced himself to smile. "I'm just not into cutting up frogs."

Ed kept making small talk, but none of it interested me much. My attention stayed fixed on Cat. She chewed her lip and wrote in her notebook. No one at her table spoke to her, and she didn't do anything with the dissection. She seemed even more isolated than Dan.

At one point, Dan walked behind her to get some paper towels, and I glimpsed what she'd been writing. Instead of lab notes, she cupped in her hand a carefully folded page with a name written on the front in curly, elegant letters: *Finn.*

Dan glanced at the table where the guy with the lazy smile who'd been nice to Teagan sat. So that must be Finn. The zombie watched him intently. He looked above average in height, with perfectly symmetrical, attractive features, yet from a strictly physical perspective, Dan might be considered more handsome. And although Finn dressed well enough, his sense of style wasn't exactly original. The thing that struck me the most about him was his confident, friendly manner. While other students were insecure and self-conscious, Finn appeared at ease and in control.

There were three other people in Finn's lab group—an obnoxious, geeky guy with curly hair; an awkward girl with thick glasses; and a pretty blonde whom I'd noticed with Finn before. I'd thought Finn might just talk to the blonde, but he involved everyone in his group.

I tried to block out the other noises in the classroom so I could hear what he said. The curly-haired guy was manipulating their frog's legs, making it do a grotesque little dance on a folder.

"Nice, but you're freaking out the ladies," Finn said.

Curly smiled sheepishly and set their frog back down.

Finn turned to the girl with glasses, who'd pushed her stool back from the table. "It's all right if you don't want to do the dissection," he told her. "You can be note taker."

She looked relieved and scooted her stool closer.

Once their frog was pinned to the wax board, Finn passed a scalpel to the blond girl. "Care to start the incision, Nurse?"

The blond girl paled. "Uh . . . no, thanks, Doctor," she replied. "You can do it."

"If you insist." Finn took the scalpel and cut into the frog. "Forceps," he said, holding his hand out to the blonde. She passed him the scissors, happy to play along.

It went on like that for some time, with Finn directing while the others followed his lead. I couldn't hear everything he said, but everyone in his group seemed to enjoy being a part of the game. Students at nearby tables kept looking over, like they wished they could join his group. I didn't blame them. It certainly looked more fun than what was going on in any other group. Even the teacher spent most of his time hanging around Finn's table.

"What do you think, Mr. Huber?" asked Finn at one point. "Is our patient going to make it?"

"The prognosis isn't favorable," replied Mr. Huber.

"Ah, but we have a mad scientist on our team," said Finn, nodding at the curly-haired guy.

Curly held up a frog organ and squeezed it, much to the girls' disgust.

"Easy, Igor," said Finn. "The cafeteria needs that."

Cat kept watching Finn during class. I sank deeper into Dan, feeling his whispers churn with angry tones. Was he jealous? I thought of the note I'd seen Cat writing. Then it hit me, with the proverbial force of a cannonball to the gut — Cat liked Finn.

That evening, after stuffing himself with frozen pizza for dinner, the zombie grew restless. He told his mom he had to meet someone to study for a test, but the kid was such a loser he couldn't even think of a decent lie when she asked him what subject it was for.

"Uh . . . it's just a test," he said.

"Whatever," replied his mom, too tired to question him further. "It's your life. Do what you like. Just remember, tomorrow's a school day."

You'd think, with wide-open permission like that, the zombie would do something interesting. For a good twenty minutes, though, he merely drove around, listening to music. I squirmed, wishing he *did* need to meet someone to study. Anything seemed better than being stuck alone with him. Finally, Dan drove back to town, turned onto a familiar street, and pulled over four doors down from Cat's apartment.

I perked up at the prospect of seeing Cat, but he didn't get out of the car. Instead, he switched off the headlights and stared at her window. I tried urging him to walk to her apartment, only it didn't work. He just sat in the car, watching her place. The lights in her room eventually flicked off, and she stepped out her front door, heading the opposite direction from where Dan had parked. When she reached the end of the block, she turned away from town.

Dan started his car and edged forward, keeping his headlights off. After a few blocks, he must have thought his car would give him away because he shut off the engine and slipped out. Then he continued after Cat on foot, staying hidden behind bushes and trees. Score one for the zombie — this time, at least, he managed to be a little stealthy.

Cat followed a narrow road. There weren't any streetlamps overhead, and the houses became more spread out, occupying wide overgrown lots. She turned onto a dirt driveway that led to an old farmhouse with boarded-up windows. The porch roof dipped, and some of the walls slanted, giving the whole structure a whimsical slouch.

Dan knelt behind a bush across the street and watched as Cat entered through a side door. She must have lit a few candles, because a flickering glow soon leaked through the cracks in the boards covering the windows. A few minutes later, a car pulled up in front of the house. The driver's door swung open and Finn stepped out.

Immediately, Dan's pulse quickened. Sweat trickled down his arms, and his mouth grew dry. I sank deeper into him, but I couldn't discern what he was thinking. He'd become more agitated than I'd ever seen him — his incomprehensible whispers heaving and churning like rapids in a river. I pulled back, disturbed by the turmoil.

As soon as Finn went into the house, Dan darted across the street and crouched near the door Finn had gone through. The beat of the zombie's heart grew louder.

"You here?" called Finn.

Cat gave a response, only I couldn't make out what

it was. Dan crawled closer, pushing open the door. He peered into a dingy kitchen. Candles flickered on the countertops, but I didn't see Finn or Cat. Their voices came from a room to the left.

"Nice place," said Finn. "Anyone else here?"

"No," answered Cat. "We're alone."

Finn didn't say anything for several seconds. When he spoke again, his voice sounded confident and in control, the way he'd been during the frog dissection. "I like how you've painted the place," he said. "It's festive. So what did you want to talk about?"

"Us."

"Really?" Finn paused. "Look, I'm flattered, Cat. Truly, I am. But I don't think it's going to work out."

"Then why did you come here?"

"Courtesy," he said. "I care about you."

"Will you sit?" she asked.

The floorboards creaked as someone moved.

Cat waited before continuing. "I want you to tell me something. Tell me . . ." Her voice tightened. "Tell me what I meant to you."

There was a long silence. Had they broken up? Was Cat trying to win him back? I desperately wanted to see if she looked angry or upset. Dan pushed the door open farther, but I could only make out shadows in the flickering light. The house smelled strongly of candles and spray paint.

"What you meant to me?" Finn replied. "All right. I'll admit I enjoyed our time together. But you have to let go of this fantasy that things meant more than they did."

"You're lying," she said.

"I'm not," said Finn. "I know you want to believe that we shared something special."

"Stop lying!" she said.

The zombie's fingers dug into the wooden floor, and his stomach lurched.

"Shhh . . ." soothed Finn. "You can't change this. I just don't feel the same way about you that you do about me."

"You will."

Dan edged forward until he saw her. Cat was standing, holding a candle, while Finn reclined on the couch. Then Dan shifted to get a better view and the floor creaked.

Cat turned. She looked bewildered when she saw Dan and not at all pleased. "What are you doing here?"

The zombie scrambled to his feet. "I . . ." he stammered. Blood rushed to his face.

"You're not supposed to be here," she said.

Say something, I urged, but his words died in his throat. He couldn't even meet Cat's gaze, so he focused on Finn instead. "Leave Cat alone."

Finn gave Dan a bemused smile. "Leave her alone? What exactly do you think's going on here?"

Dan grabbed Finn by his shirt, yanking him off the couch. *"Leave!"* he repeated through clenched teeth.

"Stop it!" yelled Cat. "Let him go."

The strength drained out of the zombie's arms. He turned to her, brow knotted. "Cat, you're confused—"

"Please, just let him go."

"I'm trying to protect you."

"Don't you get it?" said Finn, pulling free of Dan's grasp. He reached into his back pocket and drew out a folded slip of paper. It was the note I'd seen Cat write in biology class. "She invited me here."

Dan looked from Finn to Cat. "Why?" There was something so raw and desperate in his voice, even I felt bad for him. *Why Finn and not me?* he seemed to be asking.

Cat didn't reply.

"I know what this is about," said Finn. "You think you can jump me away from school. You think this will make you feel better." He shook his head, disappointed. "I thought we were cool, Dan. I tried to be your friend."

Dan's thoughts raged around me, making me worry about what he might do.

"It's not too late," continued Finn. "I'm still willing to forgive you." He held out his hand.

Take it, I thought.

Dan charged. It was such a spastic, clumsy attack that all Finn had to do was pivot like a matador and Dan stumbled past, smacking into a wall.

Pain exploded around me, bright as the desert sun. I recoiled, avoiding the sensation. Dan tried to punch Finn, but his fist glanced off Finn's shoulder. Finn countered with a blow to Dan's chest. The two of them kept fighting, only things felt duller now. Distant.

For Dan, the fight might have taken on a sort of slow-motion clarity, but for me it was like watching a poorly filmed action sequence with the camera jerking from the ceiling, to Cat's shirt, to an empty milk jug, to a clenched fist. Dan swung blindly, and his forearm cracked Finn's jaw. It was a lucky hit, sending Finn staggering back. Then Dan tackled Finn and the two of them skidded across the dusty floor into the couch.

Dan attempted to choke Finn, while Finn shoved the zombie's head to the side. In the candlelight, I glimpsed a giant turtle painted on the wall. I only saw it for an instant before Finn's hand crossed Dan's face. I couldn't see Cat, but I heard her.

"Dan, stop!" she screamed. "You have to stop!"

A thin, heady smell filled Dan's senses. He shifted to get a better hold on Finn and kicked over some candles.

Instantly, the couch whooshed into flames. The heat

stunned me. I thought Dan's hair had caught fire. He leaped back, brushing his head with his hands, but he seemed okay.

Finn scrambled away from the burning couch. "What the hell?" He kept backing up, looking from Dan to Cat as if he couldn't believe what had happened. "You're crazy. Both of you are crazy."

Dan grabbed a board and tried to beat out the flames with it, which ended up being worse than useless. Sparks shot onto the floor and wall. Pretty soon, the whole couch was burning and flames swept the ceiling. In the sudden light, I glimpsed giant mushrooms, rose vines, teacups, flamingos, and other odd images on the walls, until the acrid smoke grew thick and Dan's vision blurred.

He turned to survey the room. Finn must have left. Only Cat remained, standing close enough to the burning couch to roast marshmallows on it.

"We have to get out of here," Dan said with his typical flair for stating the obvious.

Cat kept staring at the flames.

"Cat!" Dan shouted.

Still no reaction. He grabbed her wrist and dragged her to the door—or at least to where the door might be. It was hard to see anything now.

He bumped into the kitchen counter and felt along the cabinets, clutching Cat's arm in his other hand. At last they made it out, but Dan still wouldn't let go. He led her down the driveway. Cat resisted. I was afraid she might run back into the house. Did Finn mean so much to her that she'd rather die than be without him?

Dan doubled over, coughing. When he could stand again, Cat was several steps away, staring at the house.

Smoke poured between the cracks in the boards on the windows and under the front door. A few flames licked through a broken window by the porch. Once the fire reached outside, things spread quickly. Flames climbed the shutters, skipping along shingles to the roof. Dan began to curse. "We have to go," he said.

Cat didn't reply.

Sirens wailed in the distance. "The cops are coming." He tugged her arm. "Cat, come on."

Cat looked at him, orange light glinting off her eyes. "You ruined it," she said. "It's all ruined."

The sound of a screen door slamming rang out from across the street. Dan glanced over, spotting movement on a porch and the glow of a phone.

When he turned back, Cat was running across the field next to the burning house. Dan sprinted after her, but after a block he must have remembered his car because he slowed.

"Cat!" He seemed torn between chasing her and fetching his car.

She kept going. After what he'd done—wrecking her meeting with Finn, attacking him, starting the fire— I couldn't blame her for running away. A police cruiser roared past, and more sirens pierced the quiet dark. Dan finally made up his mind and sprinted back to the road. He ducked into his car, started the engine, and pulled onto a side street.

His vision wavered with every squeeze of his heart. I think he was searching for Cat, but he didn't find her. After a while, he gave up and drove home.

His mom was lying on the couch watching TV when he came in. He hurried down the hall, pretending not to hear her questions about where he'd been. Then he locked himself in the bathroom and doused his head in the sink. He washed his face and hands several times. Still, the smell of smoke wouldn't leave.

Night

By the time the zombie settled down and lost consciousness, it was late.

"Took you long enough," said TR the moment I slipped out. "I've been waiting forever for you."

"I have to find Cat," I said, rushing past him.

"Nice to see you, too, dude."

I explained that the zombie had burned down a house and I needed to see if Cat was all right.

TR's eyebrows lifted. "That sounds better than my day."

★   ★   ★

We found Cat curled up in bed. Her eyes were closed, and she kept making this low, strangled, whimpery sound, but I couldn't see any sign of an injury.

"What's wrong with her?" asked TR.

"I don't know," I said. "I think she lost something."

TR frowned. "Like what? A puppy?"

I thought of Finn, only I didn't want to say that was it. Then I remembered the self-portrait she'd destroy tomorrow. "I think she lost herself," I said. "I think that's why I'm supposed to save her."

TR gave me a perplexed look. "Dude, how do you know that's what you're *supposed* to do?"

"Because the zombie messed things up for her," I said. "So I need to change things."

"How?" pressed TR.

"That's what I have to figure out."

"But how do you know that's what you're *supposed to do*?" he repeated.

I wasn't ready to tell TR about the message carved into Dan's wall. He'd probably question it or claim it could mean anything. "There has to be a reason I'm here."

TR snorted and drifted about Cat's room, kicking a pile of smoky clothes on the floor. His foot went right through them, not moving a thread.

"This is boring," he said after a while. "Let's jump off a building."

Cat shuddered. I knelt by her, afraid that I'd let her down. What if I was supposed to stop Dan from going into the house and ruining her chances with Finn, and I'd already failed? "I think I'll stay here."

"Whatever." TR looked disappointed. "I'll find you tomorrow. Or yesterday. Or whatever it is." He paused before stepping out and smirked at me. "Good luck trying to save her, dude."

Wednesday, November 12

When Dan woke the next morning, the wound on his forehead looked worse. It was like watching a black spot on a banana grow. The faint yellow-and-blue tinge of the bruise had spread around the oblong scab. I probably shouldn't have been eager to find out how Dan had gotten injured—especially since I'd feel it, too—but I couldn't help being curious. The wound looked bigger than I'd initially thought. It might have been healing for a week or two to get to this point. For all I knew, someone really *had* smacked him with a shovel. But who? And why?

Dan tried, with little success, to get his hair to cover

the wound. He ended up wearing a baseball cap to break-fast. The rim of the cap grated against the scab, which sent a jolt of pain through him every now and then — a brisk reminder that the wound was still there.

Teagan greeted him with her usual silent treatment at breakfast. She asked their mom to take her to school again. After some discussion, their mom finally agreed, but not without commenting on how it would make her late. No wonder Teagan felt like a burden.

"Your brother still goes to school, doesn't he?" quipped their mom.

"Unfortunately," said Teagan.

"Is there something going on between you two?"

Good question, I thought, wondering how Dan would field this one, but the zombie simply froze, spoon poised halfway to his mouth.

Teagan looked at him, then glanced away. "No."

His shoulders relaxed.

"It's just so hard to follow in my big brother's foot-steps," continued Teagan with a heavy dose of sarcasm.

"Oh, well," said their mom. She gave Teagan a thin smile. "You'll have to make your own footsteps, then. Right?"

Teagan rolled her eyes and headed to the car.

After downing the rest of his breakfast, Dan returned to his room. He looked at the calendar, with its lame advice on courage. Then he lifted up the bottom half, as he'd done the other day. I almost didn't read the words etched in the wall since I already knew what they'd tell me. SAVE HER. But what if I couldn't save her? What if I'd missed my opportunity?

FEAR WILL CAUSE WHAT YOU FEAR

At first, I didn't believe his eyes. Dan dragged his fingers over the words, feeling the coarse scratches in the drywall that formed them. This wasn't possible. There hadn't been anything else etched into the wall before — no crossed-out words or spackle filling in previous messages. The calendar was in the exact same place where it had been, or would be. So how on earth could the message have changed? It was carved into the wall, for God's sake.

He released the calendar and made sure it covered the words. That was the other strange thing — Dan didn't act the least bit surprised that the message had changed. Then again, in his world, maybe it hadn't changed at all.

School that morning passed in an uneasy blur. I kept thinking about the new message, and what it could mean.

The only thing I knew for sure was that things were different. Something I'd done had caused the zombie's past to shift, if only slightly. How else could words carved into a wall transform? So maybe the messages were clues about what I should do. It would have been nice, though, if the clues could have been more specific. For all I knew, "Fear will cause what you fear" meant that my aversion to mucus would cause the zombie to pick his nose.

Things didn't get interesting at school until after lunch, when Dan went to biology class. He sat in a different seat from the one he'd sat in the other day and stole glances at the door while pretending to draw in his notebook. At last, Cat walked in, wearing a green skirt, striped tights, and a purple long-sleeved T-shirt with black cats on it. I loved her style. While everyone else dressed like dull imitations of store mannequins, Cat wasn't afraid to be wholly original.

She sat near the front of the room, which was also different. Once class started, Mr. Huber read names off a list and pointed to tables where students were supposed to go for their lab groups. I already knew where everyone would end up.

After students settled into their "new" seats, Mr. Huber lectured about proper dissection techniques and how lucky they were to get to work with *real* frogs tomorrow. He threatened a pop quiz on the five main systems of the body if people didn't pay attention, but I knew he was bluffing. He'd dedicate the whole period tomorrow to slicing open frog bellies and scolding students for chucking livers and eyeballs at one another.

Dan surreptitiously watched Cat during class, but her

attention stayed fixed on Finn. He sat at the table in front of her now, whispering to Kendra—the blond girl in his lab group.

The muscle on the side of Cat's jaw flexed as she watched Kendra and Finn together. At one point, Finn turned in his seat and noticed Cat staring. He gave her a warm, welcoming smile, as if he'd been waiting all day to see her and no one else mattered. He even winked, but Cat didn't wink back. She looked upset. Did she think Finn was flirting with Kendra?

I remembered the conversation I'd overheard in the house and how Finn would tell Cat that he didn't feel the same way about her that she did about him. And now here he was, winking at her. No wonder she was confused.

Later, when Kendra went to sharpen her pencil, she slowed by Cat's table. "Give it up," she said, in a voice loud enough for half the class to hear. "He'll never be interested in a freaky slut like you."

Before I could see Cat's reaction, Mr. Huber called Dan to the front to get his group's lab assignment. He passed behind Cat on the way back. She looked pale and forlorn. *It's not true,* I wanted to tell her. *You're better than Kendra. You're better than all of them.* But Dan said nothing

What if I'm supposed to help Cat win over Finn? I wondered. *That could be the way to save her.*

The thought tormented me. Finn seemed like a great guy. I could understand why Cat liked him, but how was I supposed to help them be together? Even if I could influence Dan into doing that, why would he? And why would I, since I wanted to be with her myself? It wasn't fair. Then again, if I was too selfish or jealous to help her, something bad might happen to Cat. Like the wall said, fear of losing her could cause her to be lost.

It wasn't until last period, during history class, that I got to see Cat again. Mrs. Pepper let Dan go to the library to work on a research project. It was my first time in the library, and the place brightened my mood. The zombie barely looked up, but the room felt airy and open — a pleasant change from the claustrophobic cinder-block classrooms.

Dan leaned over a sign-in sheet on the front desk and wrote his full name, *Dan Franklin,* followed by the time, class, and the reason for his visit. Then he checked the other names signed in, spotting *Cat Slater* a few lines above his.

She's here! I thought, sinking deeper into Dan. I focused on urging him to look for her.

Several tables occupied the center of the room, but Cat wasn't working at any of them. Dan glanced at the sign-in sheet again. She'd only arrived five minutes before, and the "Time Out" column was blank, so she must still be in the library.

Dan wandered the perimeter, checking study carrels while pretending to search for a book.

"Can I help you find something?" asked Mrs. Gilbert, the librarian.

"No," he mumbled. "I'm good." He slid out an over-sized volume wrapped in plastic and held it up for Mrs. Gilbert to see.

"Take a seat, please," she said. "This isn't a gym."

Dan glanced around the library one last time and shuffled to an empty table near the exit. Smart. Cat would have to walk by him to leave. He leaned back and pretended to read the book he'd chosen. *The Heroes of D-Day.* A black-and-white photo of soldiers charging up a beach graced the cover. He thumbed through the pages, pausing at some of the pictures: young men, packed into boats, looking scared and seasick; soldiers wading through breaking waves, holding their rifles above their heads; other soldiers, crawling over corpses to get a little farther up the beach. Maybe he wanted to be like the men in the photos, risking his life for a cause, and that's why he'd followed Cat into the house. The soldiers were nearly the same age as him. And like so many of the men in the book, he'd die an early death. Only for what?

More students filtered into the library. They huddled around the sign-in sheet, whispering and snickering. Kendra, Bella, and Laney—three popular juniors I'd seen together in a few of Dan's classes—were among them. Dan buried his head in his book, trying to ignore them.

It was hard to ignore their whispers, though. After a few minutes, I got the sense that they were talking about Dan. He stared at a photo of a makeshift grave marker consisting of a soldier's helmet perched on a gun, but his eyes wouldn't focus. Every time he glanced up, people looked away.

Finally, near the end of the period, Cat emerged from the stacks. A hush descended on the room as she strode to the front desk to check out some books. *There she is,* I whispered. *Go talk to her.*

Dan fidgeted and his pulse quickened. He ducked behind the book, watching as Cat leaned over the sign-in sheet. Then her face fell slack, and she dropped the clipboard. The board hit the desk with a smack that echoed through the room.

Someone stifled a laugh.

Cat hurried toward the exit, leaving her books behind.

Say something, I urged. *This is your chance.*

Cat passed Dan, not even looking at him. She was already to the door.

Come on!

"Wait," Dan sputtered. I think he meant to whisper, only it came out much louder. Several students giggled.

Dan edged between Cat and the door. "I need to talk to you," he said. "It's important."

"Don't." Cat bit her lip and glanced over her shoulder. More people seemed to be watching. "Don't do this now."

He kept blocking the door. "I just want to talk."

"*Slut!*" coughed Kendra.

Bella and Laney coughed words as well, as if it were a sick competition to see who could say *slut* the most.

Cat's jaw trembled. I realized their insults were directed at her.

Dan reached for her. "Cat—"

"Leave me alone!" She pushed past him and hurried into the hall.

Dan seemed about to go after her when Mrs. Gilbert's voice cut across the room. "Dan Franklin!" she called. "Aren't you forgetting something?"

He glanced back, confused.

"You need to return your book to the reshelving cart and sign out," said Mrs. Gilbert. Then she glared at the center tables, where students were still fake-coughing. "Is something going on here?"

"No, Mrs. Gilbert," said Bella. She cleared her throat. "It's just allergies."

Mrs. Gilbert nodded, satisfied that the students were quieting down. I couldn't believe it. She *knew* — everyone knew — that Kendra and Bella and the others were taunting Cat, but no one said a word to stop it.

Sweat rolled down Dan's sides. He put his book away and strode to the main desk to sign out. When he saw the clipboard, he froze.

Someone had changed his last name on the sign-in sheet from *Franklin* to *Frankenstein*. And they'd changed Cat's name to *Cat-Lip*. Next to this, filling the margins of the sheet, was a crude drawing of the Frankenstein monster, complete with head wound, embracing a girl with an exaggerated scar on her lip.

People had written things around the figures like *Bride of Frankenstein* and *slut whore*. There were worse names scrawled there, but I had trouble reading them. Dan's eyes blurred, and a nauseating mixture of anger and pain made his chest ache. It looked like everyone who'd signed in had added something cruel to the page.

He tore off the sign-in sheet and crumpled it in his hand. Several people burst out laughing, but the blood rushed so hard through Dan's head, it was difficult to hear them. He marched to Kendra's table.

"Frankenstein angry," quipped Bella.

Kendra looked up, feigning innocence. "Did your girl-friend leave already? I guess she's only interested in guys who are still on the team."

The zombie clenched his jaw and glared at her, but what could he say? He was the reason they were taunting Cat, and the more he defended her, the worse he'd make things.

"Are you going to fight me, Frankenstein?" Kendra teased.

"Who took the sign-in sheet?" asked Mrs. Gilbert.

"I think Dan has it," replied Kendra, the picture of politeness.

"Dan?" Mrs. Gilbert frowned at him.

He gripped the balled-up sheet in his fist and headed for the door.

"Dan Franklin!" called Mrs. Gilbert. "Get back here!"

Dan continued walking. For once, I felt just as mute as him.

Dan ended up staying for detention after school. Mrs. Gilbert asked him why he'd taken the sign-in sheet, but he refused to speak. Whatever existed between him and Cat, he wasn't going to tell any teachers about it.

"So you're interested in D-day?" she asked, trying a different approach. She sat across from him at one of the center tables. "Is that for a project?"

"No."

"Personal interest, then?"

He shrugged.

Mrs. Gilbert kept folding and unfolding her hands. "Do you know what courage is?" she asked.

Doing something stupid and running like hell, I thought, recalling the inspirational message on Dan's calendar.

"Courage is doing what's right even when you know it will make your life harder," continued Mrs. Gilbert. "It's never easy to show courage like that, but it's better than the alternative."

I drifted closer to Dan, intrigued. He lifted his head and met Mrs. Gilbert's gaze.

"To paraphrase Martin Luther King Jr., the moment we stop doing what we know is right is the moment our lives begin to end." She unfolded her hands and let them flop back so her rings thumped the table. "Do you understand?"

I thought of Dan's body bleeding in the tub. Was there a point when he'd stopped doing what was right?

I nodded.

Dan nodded.

"Good." She folded her hands again. "So, are you ready to tell me *why* you took the sign-in sheet?"

Dan lowered his gaze. Bits of black gunk speckled her gold rings, darkening the crevices between the tines and diamonds. "No," he said.

"Suit yourself," Mrs. Gilbert replied. "Detention ends at five o'clock."

The only sound in the halls was the whir of the custodian's vacuum when Dan got to leave. He took the long way home, driving past the apartment complex where Cat lived. Then he pulled over a few houses down and watched her window, like he'd done the other day. If anyone had seen him, they probably would have thought he was stalking Cat, but after the incident in the library, I saw his actions differently. He wanted to do something good, only he couldn't figure out how.

Teagan was watching TV and talking on the phone when Dan got home. He went straight to his room and turned on his iPod. I hoped he'd fall asleep so I could escape for a while, but he stayed restless until dinner. Then he emerged, devoured a plate of lasagna, and retreated to his room without thanking his mom for dinner.

He got on the Internet. This time I paid attention to his searches. He looked up suicide techniques.

It's freaky what people will post under the guise of being helpful. Dan seemed familiar with some of the sites already, so I guess he'd been toying with the idea for a while. He found what he was searching for pretty quickly. I tried to avoid looking at the pictures, since I already knew more than I cared to about the subject.

Night

At last, Dan brushed his teeth and called it a day. As soon as he lost consciousness, I broke free, eager to get away from him.

I went to the Coffee Spot first, in case Cat was there. Spooner hunched in the back booth, playing with his lighter. A couple other punk kids from school occupied the bench across from him, but no Cat.

I spotted TR hanging out at a nearby table with a family. A mom, dad, teenage daughter, and a boy around ten were all sharing two slices of pie. TR saw me and winked. With elaborate gestures, he pretended to devour a bite of peach pie on the teenager's fork.

"You're here early," I said.

TR slid out of the booth and stood. "Waster stole a bottle of vodka from his neighbors after school. He passed out an hour ago."

"Oh. Sorry."

"Don't be, man. It means I get a big night. I'm celebrating." He pretended to pick up a glass and raise it.

"Celebrating what?"

"Today I made Waster stick his pinkie in an automatic pencil sharpener," TR announced.

"Really?"

"Yeah. He screamed like a little girl. It was flipping hilarious."

"Hold on," I said. "What do you mean you *made* him to do it?"

"Like I took over for a second and made him jam his pinkie into the little hole."

"How?"

"It was just the tip of his pinkie."

"I mean, how exactly did you take over for a second?"

TR drifted to an empty table and waited for me to sit. "That's the weird part, dude," he said. "You know how sometimes you can get close and suggest something to them? And then they do it, and you don't know if it's a coincidence or not?"

I nodded, thinking of how I'd urged Dan to look for Cat in the library.

"Well, this time I got so close that I noticed a gap."

"A gap?"

"It's like there were all his thoughts, and then there were the things his body did," TR explained, holding his hands a few inches apart. "And between them, there was this tiny gap. So I slipped into the gap, and instead of just suggesting things to him, I grabbed the reins and took over."

"Wow." I leaned back. This changed everything.

"It didn't last," he continued. "Once the pencil sharpener bit his pinkie, he shoved me out of the way and regained control. But for a second I was right there, steering the ship." TR grinned. "You should have seen it."

I thought of what I'd do if I could take over the zombie, even for an instant. My gaze shifted to a group of people coming in the door.

"You're looking for that weird chick, aren't you?"

"Maybe."

"Dude, you're obsessed," he said.

"I told you, she's why I'm here. I'm supposed to save her."

"That again?" He chuckled. "You know what I'm supposed to do?"

I shook my head.

"Get Waster to sharpen his pinkie," he said.

I laughed, which felt good since I hadn't laughed all day. The zombie almost never laughed.

We hung out in the diner for a while, but when Cat still didn't show, I wanted to try her place. TR offered to come. On the way, I asked him if he ever wondered why he got stuck in Waster and not someone else.

"Beats me," he said. "Why does anyone get born as who they are? I mean, people don't get to choose their family. Or their body. Or their gender, right? It just happens."

"I guess." TR never seemed to get tangled up in the big unanswerable questions. He just accepted things and went with it. Sometimes I wished I could do that. Still, I couldn't accept that it was all merely chance. There had to be a *reason* I'd gotten stuck with Dan. Maybe it had something to do with him killing himself. Or maybe it was because he was empty—the closest empty vessel to Cat. "At least Waster has friends," I mused. "Everyone hates the zombie."

"Yeah. Well, I bet the zombie doesn't puke on himself. Believe me, it's no fun riding out the spins."

"The zombie bites his nails and scratches his cheek with the chewed-off ends," I said.

"Waster plucks his eyelashes and brushes his lips with them," TR replied.

"The zombie smells his shoes before he puts them on."

"Waster smells his pits when no one's looking."

"The zombie licks the sugar off donuts before eating them."

"Waster licked his math book and gave himself a paper cut on his tongue."

"No way."

"Way," said TR sticking out his tongue. "Right *dere*," he added.

We kept trading stories about our corpses. It was funny—there were so many little things we knew about them that no one else noticed, but a lot of the things we shared were similar. I found that oddly comforting.

When we got to Cat's place, TR let me step through the wall first. It took a few seconds for my eyes to adjust to her room. The curtains were drawn, and the only illumination came from a few candles on her desk and the Christmas lights strung across the purple ceiling. The music streaming from her computer fit the dim lighting. Cat huddled on the floor, looking through old photo albums. Seeing that she wasn't naked, I stuck my arm through the wall and signaled for TR to come in. It meant a lot to me that he'd waited.

TR drifted around the room, then knelt by Cat to see what she was doing. Every now and then, she pulled a photo out of the album and set it in a stack. She had a metal bowl in front of her full of ripped-up photos.

"Dude," said TR. "She's destroying her kiddie pictures. That's messed up."

"Not all of them," I said, looking closely at the pictures she'd chosen. "Just the ones that show her scar."

TR leaned closer and studied the torn photos in the bowl. "That scar on her lip? What's the big deal?"

Cat-Lip, I thought, recalling the crude drawing of her as the bride of Frankenstein on the sign-in sheet. I wondered if kids had always teased her for this one small flaw. Then again, it had probably never seemed small to her.

"If I had an album like that, I sure as hell wouldn't destroy it," TR said.

A few of the photos she pulled out looked like they'd been taken in a hospital. She seemed maybe nine or ten in the pictures, although it was hard to tell because there were bandages on her face. In one, she was giving the camera a thumbs-up, probably because she couldn't smile.

"Maybe she wants to forget," I said.

"Forget what?"

"Her past. The way people used to treat her."

"If you forget your past, then who are you?"

"We don't have a past," I pointed out. "At least not one we remember."

"Whatever, dude. This is depressing." TR backed away. "I'm going to wait outside."

"You don't have to wait for me."

"What else am I going to do? Get smashed by a truck?" He shrugged. "I'll wait."

After TR left, I watched Cat tear some pictures out of her yearbooks. She started with middle school. She wasn't smiling in any of these. Instead, she kept her mouth as flat and ordinary as possible. When she got to her freshman-year photo, she looked different again. She must have had another surgery, and her scar was like it was now — a small, jagged line above her top lip. She smiled in this photo, only it wasn't the wide, unself-conscious smile she'd had as a child.

Cat held up one last photo of herself as a seven- or eight-year-old kid, dressed as a clown for Halloween. A woman knelt next to her. They were hugging and making goofy faces. The woman's eyes reminded me of Cat's. She'd appeared in a few earlier pictures, yet not any later ones. It could have been her mom. I remembered what Dan had said the other day about how he and Cat used to go to group counseling sessions years ago, and she was the only one who got what he was going through. So maybe her mom had done something similar to Dan's dad and left to start a new family.

In the picture, Cat looked happy. She was holding a bright-orange plastic jack-o'-lantern. Her cheeks were painted white, and her mouth had been outlined in red. Her mom wore red clown makeup, too, and both of them were scrunching their noses and sticking out their tongues as they smiled.

Cat took a candle from her desk and set it on the floor by the bowl of torn photos. Then she held the Halloween photo up by the flame, studying it.

No. Keep this one, I told her.

My words made no difference. Cat moved the picture over the candle until the corner caught fire. She turned it, letting the flames creep up the side and singe her fingers before she dropped it into the bowl with the others. The photos curled and smoked, then turned black. Orange light reflected off her eyes, same as when she'd stared at the burning house. She carried the bowl to the window, switched on her fan, and blew the smoke outside.

I hated seeing her destroy her past. More than anything, I think she wanted to be accepted. Not to conform, like everyone else, but to be herself and not be rejected. So I stayed with her and whispered to her. Even if it was pointless, I told her that she was beautiful and that she'd always been beautiful, until she lay down and closed her eyes.

When I finally left, I found TR sitting on the curb in front of her house.

"She asleep?" he asked.

I nodded.

"Good," he said. "Now let's find something crazy high to jump off of."

We climbed a radio tower at the edge of town. I followed TR up it without looking back. I figured I owed him for waiting for me. After at least ten minutes of climbing, we reached the red light at the top, and I glanced down. The ground loomed so far below that the houses looked tiny, and I could feel the tower sway. Panic gripped me. I clung to the metal rungs, cursing myself for going so high.

"You afraid?" asked TR.

"Hell, yes," I said. "Aren't you?"

"Not of falling," he said. "I'm more afraid of *not* falling."

I realized that was it exactly. Beneath the ordinary fear of smacking the ground lurked this deeper, more disconcerting fear. What if I didn't fall? What if I just floated away and detached from everything?

"Fear will cause what you fear," I said, reciting the message etched into the wall.

"Then we better not chicken out," replied TR. "On three?"

I nodded.

"One . . . two . . . three!"

I shut my eyes and let go.

At first, I thought my fear of floating away had come true, because the wind didn't rush past my ears. In fact, nothing seemed to change. But when I opened my eyes, I saw the metal rungs of the radio tower drifting by slowly.

I looked up at the stars in the black sky above. Then I turned and looked down at the lights twinkling in the distance like a whole other universe of stars below. Each one was a streetlamp. A neighborhood. A home. A car. A family. A person. I thought of Cat sleeping beneath one of those lights. And the zombie. And Teagan. The more I imagined people beneath the lights, the more they called to me, sure as gravity. I started to fall faster. The rungs of the radio tower drifted by at a walking pace. Then a jog. The ground below grew larger and more defined.

"Yeeeee-haaaaa!" yelled TR. He fell face-first with his arms spread wide, like he wanted to hug the ground. "Holy freaking balls, this rules!"

I kept falling.

Hills, rocks, sand.

Trees, leaves, grass.

Father, mother, sister.

Teagan, Dan, Cat . . .

"Yes!" shouted TR once he touched down. "That was awesome!" He grinned at me. "Want to go again?"

We climbed the tower a few more times. We had to keep jumping to see what called us back.

*   *   *

By the time the stars dimmed and the sky started to lighten, I almost looked forward to returning to the zombie. After all, this might be my chance to change things. Yesterday is a new day.

TR and I split up at the cutoff to Dan's house. He paused at the end of the block. "Look for me in school," he said.

"How will I know it's you?"

TR's eyes crinkled as he flashed his goofy, lopsided grin. "You'll know," he said. "I'll make sure of it."

Tuesday,
November 11

From the moment the zombie woke up, I tried to make him do things. Following TR's advice, I sank into Dan until his thoughts surrounded me. I couldn't make out what went through his head, yet I could feel all these whispers brushing against me and tugging at my being like currents in a river. Then I found it— a quiet space between him and the world. A gap.

I slipped into the space, feeling more connected to Dan's senses than ever. He continued shaving, the tiny vibrations of the electric razor tight against his skin. *Your nose itches*, I whispered. *Scratch it.*

The zombie's hand lifted, causing the razor to snag a bump on his cheek. A sharp sting pricked his jaw. Instantly, Dan's presence snapped into place, forcing me aside. He studied where the blade had nicked him and held a tissue to the cut. I distanced myself from the pain, uncertain whether or not the zombie had raised his hand because of me.

Dan messed with his hair for a while before he gave up and left the warmth of the bathroom. He shuffled to the kitchen. I tried to find another gap. He tensed when he saw his mom, and his whispering thoughts increased, taking on an anxious tone. She had her back to him as she fiddled with the coffeemaker. He pulled a bowl down from the cabinet and filled it with his usual cornflakes. Then he opened the refrigerator to get some milk.

Orange juice, I said, sinking into a gap again. *Grab the orange juice.*

He picked up the orange juice, poured it onto his cereal, and took a hearty bite of citrus-soaked cornflakes.

Dan gagged. Immediately, he shoved me aside and took over.

"What's wrong?" asked his mom.

"Nothing," Dan grumbled, dumping his cereal out in the sink.

"Did you just waste a whole bowl?" asked his mom. She went on, ranting about how they had to make the cereal last because she wouldn't be able to go to the grocery store for a couple days, but I didn't listen. I was too busy pumping my invisible fist in the air, shouting, *Yes! Yes! Yes!*

The zombie had done exactly what I'd commanded.

For the rest of the morning, I experimented with asserting control. The more I did it, the better I got at finding gaps—small spaces that I could slip into and briefly take over. When I was in control, it was like steering a ship or driving a car. I could almost make the vehicle an extension of my thoughts while Dan zoned out in the passenger seat. But it was tricky. If I drew too much attention to myself or did something abrupt, Dan would yank the wheel out of my hands and force me back.

For instance, trying to get Dan to tell his mom he'd kill himself in four days got me immediately bumped to the backseat. The same went for attempting to make him tap-dance in the school parking lot and sing "I Feel Pretty" at the top of his lungs. And even the thought of having him write a note telling his future self how to avoid setting Cat's abandoned house on fire was enough to prevent me from getting anywhere near the wheel for almost an hour.

Basically, if I went along with Dan's expectations—driving down streets at a somber, law-abiding pace—then his presence withdrew. He even seemed to drift off a few times, taking a backseat and spacing out while I took charge. I managed a few five- or ten-minute stretches where I did everything without opposition, until I got cocky and took a wrong turn, raising my hand in class to answer one of Mr. Shepherd's questions or telling the person next to me there'd be a quiz tomorrow so they should do the reading (that one got me bumped out before I even finished the sentence). Every time I lost control, I'd get tossed around in Dan's incomprehensible thoughts until I managed to put some distance between us.

The whole process was exhausting, and after a few periods of working at it, I needed a rest. By lunchtime, though, I felt ready to try again.

The first thing I noticed, as I sank into Dan, was that the cafeteria made him even more anxious today than usual. His whispers sounded like a swarm of crazed bees. Perhaps he worried about people making fun of him, the way they would in the library. He scanned the long white cafeteria tables. Then his gaze settled on Cat, standing in one of the lunch lines, and he froze.

From the outside, he probably looked like he was doing his best zombie-in-headlights impression. His mouth gaped open, and his arms and legs locked mid-stride. But inside, his heart fluttered and his stomach twisted.

Cat got a slice of pizza and headed back to her table.

She spoke with Tricia for a few seconds, wrapped the pizza slice in a napkin, and left the cafeteria.

Follow her, I suggested. *See where she's going.*

Dan glanced at Tricia, which puzzled me. Why worry about her? Luckily, she had her back to him, which helped him make up his mind. He stepped out of line and left the cafeteria just in time to glimpse Cat turning down the portrait hall.

Don't lose her, I whispered.

Dan scuffed his heels against the floor as he walked. I sank deeper into him, searching for an opportunity to take over, but he had a pretty tight grip on the wheel.

When we got to the portrait hall, he paused and peeked around the corner. The self-portraits were all hanging, just as I remembered them, but Cat was gone. It confused me, until I noticed a door near the end of the hall that had been cracked open. Dan continued toward it. Guess he was curious, too, so I didn't need to egg him on.

A sign warned that an alarm would sound if the door was opened, but obviously, the alarm wasn't working. Dan peered through the crack at a patch of weeds growing next to the school. Then he gently pushed the door open farther. An overgrown courtyard stretched between the gym and some classrooms. He focused on a gnarled crab-apple tree near the corner. It took me a second to make out the silhouette of a person nestled against the wall behind the tree. She had her legs bent in front of her, and a book rested on her knees.

Dan held his breath, not daring to make a sound. Cat looked peaceful—more than she usually did in school. She brushed a lock of hair across her lips as she read.

"What are you doing here?" someone snapped.

Dan jerked back, letting the door slam shut. Tricia was standing in the hall behind him, looking pissed. In her hand, she cupped a pack of cigarettes. She must have been going out to meet Cat.

"Did you say something to her?" asked Tricia.

"What are you talking about?"

"I know what you're up to." Tricia glared at Dan. "If you keep harassing her, I'll call the cops. I'll tell them everything."

This must have unsettled Dan, because his presence recoiled slightly. I seized my chance, darting into the gap that had opened.

"What's there to tell?" I asked, Dan's voice echoing my thoughts.

Tricia's eyes darkened and a scowl creased her cheeks. "You're sick, you know that? I can't believe Cat actually liked you once."

"She did?" Dan slammed against me, causing my control to slip. His body twitched.

Tricia stepped closer. Even though Dan was a foot

taller than her, he backed up until his heels struck the lockers. "She doesn't like you anymore," said Tricia. "In fact, I'll make sure no one here makes that mistake again."

The bell rang, and students poured into the hallway. Tricia glanced at them, but she didn't step back. "I'm warning you," she added. "Stay away from her."

Cat didn't come to biology class that day. She must have ditched with Tricia. They missed a colorful lecture on the systems of a frog's body. While Mr. Huber talked, I kept replaying the confrontation in the hallway. Clearly, Tricia disliked Dan. I didn't blame her for being suspicious of him, although her anger seemed to go beyond ordinary disapproval. And what did she mean about Cat liking Dan once? Had they dated? If so, then all I had to do was travel backwards until Cat didn't avoid Dan or distrust him anymore. Then I could take over and talk with her. I could be with her.

A sense of possibility filled me. For the first time, being trapped in the zombie didn't seem so bad. He had potential. *We* had potential.

When the period ended, Dan grabbed his backpack and hurried for the door. He was so eager to leave that he slammed into a short, stocky guy who was entering.

"Sorry," Dan said.

"Dude, where's the fire?" replied the guy, flexing his oversized muscles.

Dan tried to step through the door, but the other guy moved at the same time, and they bumped into each other again.

"You got a problem?" asked the guy.

Dan scowled. The guy looked Hispanic. He had a thick neck and a broad, angular chest from lifting too many weights. For a moment, I thought they might get into a fight, but then Dan backed off. "Hey, I remember you," he said. "You're Terc, right?"

Waster! I thought, surprised that Dan knew him. *This is Waster.* He didn't look at all like I'd expected.

"You were fixing your truck, remember?" continued Dan.

"Damn, that's right." Waster's expression softened. "You're that crazy gringo. You find your car yet?"

"Yeah."

"That was the . . ." Terc's voice dwindled as he seemed to remember something else. "That was a weird day."

Dan nodded, and the silence became awkward. A few students piled up behind Waster, trying to get to class. Terc's cheeks suddenly dimpled with an unmistakably goofy smile. TR must have taken control. "Funny running into you here," he said.

I found a gap and hurled myself into it, taking over the zombie. "No kidding," I replied. "Quite a coincidence." Dan started to push back. I feared I'd get the boot if I said anything out of character, so I stuck to more neutral ground. "Guess I should get to class," I added.

"Guess so," he said.

I stepped back to let Waster go first, but Waster waited as well. Then, right as he started to move, I urged Dan forward.

The two of them bumped chests. It was like a high five from me to TR.

Night

"Dude, that ruled!" said TR when I met him later at the Coffee Spot. "Our corpses were like doing a tango together. Told you I'd find you."

"How'd you know who the zombie was?" I asked. I didn't think I looked like Dan, although I couldn't be sure. Riders didn't show up in mirrors. I certainly didn't feel like the zombie. He was tall and gawky—a plodding ogre of a person, while I was small, swift, and light. And, anyway, TR didn't look anything like Waster. TR had a bit of a belly, round shoulders, and a soft, laughing face, while Waster—with his bulging muscles, wide chest, and stocky build—resembled an upside-down walking triangle.

"Piece of cake," TR said. "At lunch I saw this tall dude staring at Cat and drooling so I knew you had to be in there. Then I got Waster to drink out of the wrong end of a milk carton, and he spilled milk down his shirt. Flipping hilarious, dude."

I kept an eye out for Cat while TR and I traded stories about the things we'd gotten our corpses to do. It wasn't very late—not even ten. TR and I had both managed to slip away from our corpses early. Waster had passed out after swallowing a couple pills he'd bought off a kid at school, and the zombie was so dull, he'd practically bored himself to sleep by nine. Then again, the early bedtimes could have had something to do with us. I'd certainly suggested to Dan that he lie down and close his eyes, and TR might have encouraged Waster to take the pills.

As it got closer to ten, I began to worry that Cat wouldn't show up at the diner. "Let's take a walk," I said.

"Just a walk, huh?" TR replied, grinning. He stepped through the wall and headed toward Cat's neighborhood, guessing that's where I wanted to go. I waited for him to tease me about her, but he didn't. We cut across the empty lot behind the Coffee Spot.

"Do you think we're changing their futures?" I asked.

"What do you mean?"

"When we take over and do things, do you think it changes what happens to them later?"

"Dude, I highly doubt that getting Waster to put his boxers on backwards is going to save the world."

"Maybe not. But what if we change other things?" I asked. "Things that matter."

He shrugged. "We can't change too much."

"Why not?"

"Because then we wouldn't be here." TR dragged his hand through a row of hedges. "Think about it. We both came into this existence the moment our corpses died, right? So if too much changes and the corpses don't die, then where do we go?"

"If we weren't here, then we couldn't change things," I pointed out.

TR frowned. "Now you're making my head hurt."

"Anyhow," I continued, turning onto the street where Cat lived, "I'm not talking about changing things for the corpses. I'm talking about changing things for others."

"Like weird girl?" TR asked. "The one you're *supposed* to save?"

I nodded.

"I don't know, dude," TR said. "I don't think it's easy to change stuff. Things seem pretty set, so there's no use stressing about it, you know?"

I did know. Call it fate or destiny, but I'd had the same sense that most things would happen no matter what I did. Yet that didn't mean everything was set. The fact that the message etched into Dan's wall had changed proved that things could shift. "What if they're like trains and they all have a track that they're on?" I asked.

"Train people," said TR. "Nice image. Waster watched a cartoon like that the other day."

"Just because everyone's stuck on a track doesn't mean things can't change," I continued. "Little things might change along the way. After all, every time a train goes down the track, things are slightly different. It's never exactly the same."

"The train still ends up at the same place," TR pointed out.

"Sometimes," I said. "But there could be places where a small change at exactly the right moment causes big changes down the line—the way pulling a lever can switch a train to a whole new track."

TR raised his eyebrows. "Dude, has the zombie been playing with a train set or something?"

"All I'm saying is that if I can find the right thing to change for Cat—the right lever to pull—then maybe things will be different for her."

"Maybe," conceded TR. He paused outside Cat's apartment complex. Tricia and Spooner were in the courtyard, sharing a cigarette. TR watched them for a moment, then looked at me. "So what's this lever?"

"That's what I need to figure out." I tried to hear what Tricia and Spooner were discussing.

" . . . wish my dad was a bartender," muttered Spooner as I approached. "I had to stuff my bed with pillows and climb out my window to get here."

"Boo-hoo," said Tricia. She glanced at an apartment on the second floor. "It would take my mom a week to sober up enough to notice that I'm gone."

Cat came out of her apartment a few minutes later carrying a large backpack. She asked Spooner if he had the goods. He shook his backpack, causing several cans to clank together. The three of them left the courtyard, still passing the cigarette.

"You coming?" I called to TR. He'd been ducking his head into different apartments, probably searching for naked women.

"There's a guy talking to his fish in there." He hitched his thumb at the apartment he'd just left.

I trailed behind Cat, listening to her and her friends as they headed away from town. TR goofed around, adding "in bed" to things they said, but he didn't complain or try to convince me to do something else.

After a few minutes, I figured out where they were going. Cat turned onto the road that led to the abandoned farmhouse—the one Dan would burn down. It was strange seeing it again, with its lopsided porch and crooked roof silhouetted against the moonlit sky, as if it had risen from the ashes in all its dilapidated glory.

Tricia shoved open the side door. Then she flicked her lighter and lit a couple candles on the kitchen counters. Clearly, she'd been here before. She passed one candle to Cat and kept the other.

"What if someone sees the light?" asked Spooner.

"Who?" Tricia replied. "No one comes here but us."

I studied the layout of the rooms where Dan and Finn had fought, pausing to inspect the couch that had burned. In my memory it was all destroyed, but now things looked like they'd been gathering dust here forever. And that wasn't all—something else felt different about the living room that I couldn't put my finger on.

"This is the house the zombie torched," I told TR.

"Cool," he said. "So we're like detectives at a crime scene, only the crime hasn't happened yet."

"And I know who did it," I added.

"Yeah, but do you know *why* he did it?"

"It was an accident," I said, yet that didn't feel entirely true. Dan hadn't *accidentally* followed Cat into the house. And his getting jealous and fighting with Finn hadn't been an accident, either.

TR drifted around the room. "This place looks haunted. You think there are ghosts here?"

114

"Like us?" I joked.

TR glowered. He hated being called a ghost. Still, he played along, moaning like a deranged banshee at Tricia. She didn't even blink.

"How many other people know about this place?" asked Spooner.

"Not many," said Tricia. "It's a secret. You're the only boy we've brought here."

Cat held up her candle and studied one of the walls in the living room. "We'll start here," she said.

I suddenly realized what looked different. The walls I remembered had bright, flowing scenes of rivers, mushrooms, flowers, and strange figures painted on them. So much had happened the last time I'd been here that I hadn't fully comprehended the images, but now I knew exactly what Cat was going to do.

She shrugged off her backpack and pulled out brushes, paints, and a plastic milk jug full of liquid, while Tricia lit several candles to give them light.

"This place is creepy," said Spooner. He wiped cobwebs off a stuffed animal he'd found on the floor.

"No, it isn't," said Cat. "It's sad, but we can change that."

"In bed," added TR.

I shushed him, not wanting to miss anything.

TR shook his head and wandered off.

"I didn't know what type of paints you wanted, so I grabbed a bunch," said Spooner, setting out the cans he'd brought.

"That's perfect." Cat handed Spooner a brush and another to Tricia. "Everyone gets one."

Tricia knotted her brow. "I'm terrible at painting."

"Good," said Cat. "I love terrible paintings."

"I'm serious. I can't even do stick figures."

"I can do the outlines if you want to color things in," Cat offered.

"Deal," replied Tricia.

"That sounds good to me, too," said Spooner.

Cat took a can of black paint and stared at the wall for several seconds while Tricia brought some candles over to give her more light. Without a word, Cat started to paint, using quick, fluid strokes.

"A mushroom," said Spooner, identifying the cartoon-ish outline she made. "Trippy."

"It's for the blue caterpillar," answered Cat.

"Huh?"

"Haven't you ever read *Alice's Adventures in Wonderland*?"

"I saw the movie," he replied. "Why do you like all that Alice stuff, anyway?"

Cat kept painting, moving from one image to another

without hesitation. She swiftly outlined a plump, pomp-ous caterpillar. "My mom used to read it to me."

"I thought you hated your mom."

"I hated that she left," said Cat. "When she was around, she could be fun."

TR stuck his head down through the ceiling. *"Beware the floating skull of terror!"* he moaned. Then he bobbed around like a balloon bumping against the ceiling.

"Anyhow," continued Cat, oblivious to TR's antics, "my mom would read it to me before bed, and I'd imagine that I was Alice. I could relate to her."

"Why? Did you fall down a hole?" asked Spooner.

Cat pointed to the flower she'd just painted. "That needs color," she said. "And you can add grass to the bottom."

Spooner cracked open a paint can and colored the flower red while Tricia added grass. Cat moved on to outline other stuff—trees and vines and leaves. Gradually, the walls began to resemble the ones in my memory.

"In the book, Alice is always growing and shrinking," said Cat. "She literally never fits in. She's a misfit, like me."

Tricia snorted. *"You're* not a misfit."

"Aren't I?" asked Cat.

Tricia stopped painting and propped her hands on her hips. "Do you know why Kendra and the others hate you? It's because they're afraid of you. They can't control you like everyone else. You're bigger than they are, and they know it."

"See what I mean? Bigger. Smaller. Growing. Shrinking—just like Alice."

"I don't mean physically bigger," said Tricia. "I mean you're beyond them."

Cat scoffed.

"It's true," chimed Spooner.

"Well, 'We're all mad here,'" said Cat.

Spooner looked confused.

"It's a quote—from *Alice*," Cat explained. "Anyhow, I don't want to fit in. Not anymore."

"So, what do you want?" asked Spooner.

"'A grin without a cat.'"

"A what?"

"It's another quote," said Tricia. She gestured with her brush to the crescent-shaped grin above a tree branch that Cat had just painted. "That's the Cheshire Cat, right?"

Cat nodded.

"So what's that?" asked Spooner, pointing to an oval beneath the tree branch.

"That's the Mock Turtle," she said. "He cries but has no sorrow. And this," she added, indicating the blank wall, "this is going to be the pool of tears. Alice made it when she was a giant, then she shrank and nearly drowned in it, so she wished she hadn't cried so much." Cat stepped back and studied the wall. "That's what I need to do. No more drowning in a pool of tears."

"In bed," added TR.

"Hey! You hear that?" whispered Spooner. "It sounded like footsteps."

"Maybe it's a ghost," teased Tricia.

TR and I looked at each other. "Damn straight," he said.

A floorboard creaked. Spooner and Tricia tensed.

"'Curiouser and curiouser,'" whispered Cat.

"Boo!"

Tricia cursed, but no one seemed all that surprised by Teagan's arrival. I was more stunned than any of them.

"What's up?" asked TR, noticing my reaction.

"That's the zombie's sister."

"She's cute, if you're into girls who dress like vampires."

"She's a good person," I said. Then I drifted closer to listen to their conversation.

"Didn't think you'd make it," said Tricia.

"My mom wouldn't go to sleep," answered Teagan. "And I didn't know if you'd still be here. Or if you'd want me to come."

"Did your brother see you leave?" asked Tricia.

"No. He's clueless. He barely leaves his room anymore."

TR glanced at me, arching an eyebrow.

"Don't tell him about this place," said Tricia.

"I won't," answered Teagan. "Not ever."

Cat continued to outline mushrooms by the pool of tears. She hadn't said anything to Teagan. An uncomfortable silence descended.

"If you want me to go, I will," Teagan finally said to Cat.

Cat finished the mushroom she was working on and set down her paintbrush. Then she dug through her backpack and pulled out another brush. "Who would paint the mushrooms, then?"

Teagan hesitated. "You sure?"

"Sure, I'm sure. I told Tricia to invite you."

Teagan took the paintbrush and smiled. "Thank you," she said. It surprised me how polite she acted. Around her friends, she seemed a completely different person from who she was at home. "What color should I paint them?"

"Good question." Cat studied the mushrooms on the wall. "Do you think mushrooms are happy or sad?"

"They're a fungus," said Teagan. "They eat dead things and live in the dark. Some are poisonous."

"True." Cat pursed her lips. "But some are delicious.

120

Some bring dreams and are beautiful. Some even glow in the dark."

Teagan squinted. "How about blue?" she asked. "Blue's my favorite color. Or is that too weird for mushrooms?"

"Blue's perfect," said Cat. "This is our place, so we can do whatever we like here."

"Sounds good to me," said Teagan. "I'd like to get a new family."

"Wouldn't we all," joked Tricia.

"Done," said Cat. "And this is our home."

I stayed near Cat while she outlined figures on the walls, painting over doorknobs and light switches and parts of the couch. In the candlelight, the decaying room became a work of art, as if she'd projected her dreams outside of herself and had invited us all to be part of them. A sort of reverent hush filled the room. Even TR got caught up in it. He sat for almost an hour without fidgeting and watched the paintings take shape around him.

As they worked, I thought about each of them. Tricia was the mother bear of the group—the big protector. And Spooner seemed harmless enough, if a bit of a klepto. In the short time we were there, I watched him unscrew a knob from a drawer and pocket it, along with a hair tie that Cat set down.

Teagan, the only freshman, was the youngest in the

group. Cat and Tricia were both juniors, and Spooner was a senior, although he didn't act like it. At home Teagan bristled like a wounded animal, but around Tricia and Cat, she let down her guard, happy to be adopted into their misfit tribe.

And then there was Cat. She wasn't a leader in the typical sense. She was more like a fire in a snowstorm—something radiant and improbable that they all gathered around.

Cat had just reached the third wall of the living room when Tricia announced that it was time to quit and get some sleep.

"Thanks, Mom," Teagan teased. She set down her brush and rubbed her hands together to ward off the cold.

"There's paint thinner in that jug if you want to clean the brushes," said Cat. "Actually, it's gasoline—poor man's paint thinner."

Tricia poured a little gas from the milk jug into a jar of dirty brushes while Cat added a few last details to a flamingo.

"Aren't you tired?" ask Spooner.

Cat shrugged. "I like staying awake at night. Easier to imagine things in the dark."

"Easier to steal things, too," he replied. "I snagged a case of wine from this guy's garage if you want some."

"Some other time," said Cat.

"That reminds me," continued Spooner, lowering his voice so Tricia and Teagan couldn't hear. "I asked around for that stuff you wanted. A guy I know says Trent could hook you up."

"Trent Mercer?" Cat lowered her paintbrush.

"Yeah. He's got these pills — they're not roofies, but they'll get you plenty smashed," said Spooner. "Why do you want that stuff, anyway?"

"I don't," replied Cat. "I just wanted to know."

"Know what?"

"Who has them." She set her brush in the jar and didn't paint anymore.

TR and I followed them back to the apartment complex. It was a little after two in the morning when Cat returned to her place. From the look of it, her dad still hadn't come home.

She tossed her backpack into her room and went to the bathroom to brush her teeth.

"Come on, man. You're not going to watch this, too," said TR.

"All right," I said. It looked like Cat was going to bed, anyway, and I didn't want TR to watch her undress. "Let's go."

TR jumped through the wall. I whispered, "Sweet dreams," to Cat before following him out.

We searched for people to spy on, but no one interested me as much as Cat. After an hour or so, we headed home.

I checked on Teagan when I got back to the house. She looked younger asleep. I wondered what would happen to her after Dan offed himself. If she blamed herself, she'd be devastated. And who would look out for her? Given Teagan's current relationship with their mom, I didn't think she would be much help. And her dad seemed out of the picture. So maybe Cat and Tricia would take care of her, but Cat had her own issues to deal with, and the home they'd created tonight wouldn't even be there anymore. Dan would destroy that, too.

I finally went back to his room. Except for a few lame movie posters and the calendar hanging by his bed, his walls were bare. Empty walls, empty person.

Dan rolled over in his sleep. Something pulled me toward him, but I resisted sinking back into his body. His mouth gaped halfway open, and a few creases marred his cheek. Other than that, he looked the same now as he did awake — a clumsy, hollow shell of a person sleepwalking through life. Such a waste.

Fear will cause what you fear, I thought, looking at the wall above the zombie's head. The words were hidden beneath the calendar, but that didn't matter. They'd been etched into my mind as much as the wall. Dan's fear of

124

messing up would cause him to mess up over and over again. And my fear of not being able to make things better for Cat and Teagan and Dan's mom would cause me to fail.

So if fear caused what I feared, then maybe the only solution was to be fearless. Instead of changing things in small ways, I needed to do something big and daring. I needed to take over completely, at least for a little while — then I could fix things. And why not? If I could control the zombie for a few minutes, why not a few hours? Or days? Or longer?

Granted, the notion of forcing Dan out of his life seemed questionable. But then I thought of how many people he'd hurt. His mom and sister would never recover from finding him dead in the tub, and he'd mess things up for Cat and burn down her secret house. For all practical purposes, his life was over. So what did it matter if I stepped in? I certainly couldn't make things worse. He might even thank me for taking control. And the messages did seem to be encouraging me in this direction. The only thing holding me back was fear.

I stared at his slack face and made up my mind.

From here on out, Dan's life would be mine.

Part II

Monday, November 10

YOU ARE NOT WHO YOU THINK YOU ARE

That's what I found written on the wall beneath the calendar when Dan woke up. I made him brush his hand over the letters, feeling the indentations and scratches in the drywall. He still seemed sleepy and detached. I calmed him some by pressing the calendar flat to cover the words the way I'd seen him do.

I'd watched Dan perform his morning routine enough to go through all the usual motions. To an observer, it probably looked as if nothing had changed, yet now I felt every action more intensely—the heat of the water as he showered, the steam in his lungs, the soft caress of the towel against his skin. It was glorious. The more I did, the more Dan detached. He protested a little when I began to style his hair differently, combing it into neat rows (mostly because I loved the feel of the comb on his freshly washed head), but then I brushed his hands through his hair, giving him the typical "I just woke up and don't care about style" look, and Dan settled back again.

As I dressed, I thought about the new message on the wall. The fact that it had changed this morning, right after I'd made up my mind to take over, seemed more than coincidence. It seemed like a sign. YOU ARE NOT WHO YOU THINK YOU ARE could mean I wasn't simply a rider sent here to help others. Perhaps I'd been destined to make this life mine. In time I might even get to be with Cat. I could stay with her and hold her and make her happy.

The very notion made me tremble, causing Dan's hands to fumble with his shoelaces—that's how firmly I connected to him now. The more certain I became of my purpose, the more solid my hold over his body became.

The aroma of coffee dazzled my senses when I entered the kitchen. I wanted to taste some, but I knew Dan would object. He hated coffee. Then again, if this was going to be my life, I couldn't be afraid of him. I focused on walling Dan off and keeping him detached. Then I leaned over the pot and inhaled deeply. The lush coffee smell made me think of Cat. This same scent clung to her hair and clothes.

Dan's mom came in and frowned at me.

"Good morning," I said. "Sleep well?"

She stopped in her tracks and gave me a suspicious look. "Did you break something?"

"I don't think so." I looked around for a plate or glass I might have knocked over.

"Do you need money?" she continued.

"I'm not sure," I said. "*Do* I need money?"

Dan's mom filled her coffee mug. "I don't have time for guessing games, Dan. If there's something you need to tell me, out with it."

"I just wanted to tell you good morning," I said, eager to send some positive energy her way. God knows, she needed it. "Also, I want you to have a good day. You deserve that."

She narrowed her eyes. "*What did you do?*"

"Nothing," I said. Dan grew agitated, making it harder to talk. Things were definitely not going the way I'd intended. "I simply want to express my gratitude for all that *you* do."

Her expression darkened. Did she think I was being sarcastic?

"I mean it," I added, only it came out whiny. The

more I said, the more suspicious she became. Fortunately, Teagan came in, giving her someone else to focus on.

"Are you leaving?" asked their mom. "You're not going to have breakfast?"

Teagan hoisted her backpack over her shoulder. "I'll eat something later. One of my friends is picking me up."

"Who?"

"No one you know."

"I could give you a ride," I chimed in. So far, Teagan had done her best to ignore me. "It would be my pleasure," I continued, although it was getting harder to speak. Dan pressed against me, and I had to fight to keep control.

"Are you high?" asked Teagan.

"I . . . don't think so," I stammered.

"I'm not sure I want you hopping in a car with someone I don't know," said their mom.

"It's no big deal," Teagan said. "Her name's Tricia and she's a junior, and I'm not a lesbian, so you don't have to worry about us making out and driving off a cliff."

Dan's mom scowled.

"Tricia is—" I started, but my hold slipped. I tumbled through Dan's thoughts, suddenly disconnected. Whispers swirled around me, pulling me down.

"Tricia's what?" asked Teagan. "A bitch?"

No! She's a good friend, I said. Only I wasn't able to

make Dan speak. Instead, he let out a strained "Uhhh . . ." sound.

"You're such a freak-wad."

"Teagan!" scolded their mom. "Don't swear at your brother like that."

"What? Freak-wad? *That's* swearing?"

Dan kept pushing me back. I gave in, exhausted, and let him take over. The zombie stared at his cereal. I got the sense that both Teagan and their mom expected Dan to say something, but he didn't. He just stirred the mush around.

"At least take a banana," said their mom, returning her attention to Teagan. "You need to eat something before school."

Teagan huffed and grabbed a banana before heading out.

After she left, Dan retreated to his room and calmed down a little. According to the clock by his bed, I hadn't even managed to control his body for half an hour. If I was going to take over, I had to get better at shutting Dan out. And I had to be careful not to rock the boat too much.

Dan peered inside his backpack before zipping it up. On top of his books, I noticed two figurines.

The White Rabbit.

The Cheshire Cat.

They were the exact same figurines, down to the chipped paint on the White Rabbit's pocket watch, that Cat would pull out of a shoe box four days from now. I had no idea how they'd gotten into the zombie's backpack, but I knew they meant something to Cat. So maybe I could give them to her. Thinking this renewed my sense of purpose.

I sank back into the zombie. *You are not who you think you are,* I whispered to Dan. *This isn't your life. You'll only mess things up.*

Dan looked at the calendar on the wall. I kept repeating the message written there, like a rallying cry. *You are not who you think you are.*

The message had more power than anything I could come up with on my own, because Dan had seen it, too. He knew it was real and not just some voice whispering in his head. Gradually, his battered mind soaked up the doubt I fed him and he withdrew. I slipped into the gap, making his body mine again.

I slung his backpack over my shoulder and strode to his car, eager to get to school and find Cat. Giving her the figurines could be the first step to a new relationship. Who knows? Someday Dan might even forget this life had ever been his.

★   ★   ★

At school, I did my best to follow Dan's routine, acting like he would. I kept quiet through his classes and didn't make eye contact with anyone until Dan detached so much I could barely detect him. All the while, I paid attention to every detail around me, savoring the sounds, sights, and smells of school.

By the time lunch rolled around, I felt fairly confident in my control. Dan churned a little when I spotted Cat in the hallway, but I managed to keep him at bay.

"Hi," I said, seizing the opportunity to talk with Cat.

She clenched her notebook to her chest and stared past me, waiting for someone else.

"Can we talk?" I asked.

"No." She still wouldn't meet my gaze. "There's nothing to talk about."

A serious lump formed in my throat, making it hard to speak. Any second now, I feared Dan would challenge me for control, but he remained distant. This was my chance.

"I know you don't want to see me," I started.

Cat narrowed her eyes, as if this was the biggest understatement of the year.

"But I've changed," I continued, thinking of the message on the wall. "I'm not who you think I am."

"Then, who are you?"

"Someone new. Whoever I used to be, however he — I mean *I* — messed up, I'm not that guy anymore."

"How original." She gripped her notebook tighter.

"I'm serious. Things are different now. We can start over."

Cat finally met my gaze. Perhaps she sensed some truth in my voice. "You can't just say things are different and have them be different."

"But I *am* different. You know that I am. Trust me."

"I did trust you. That's the problem, Dan."

I took a deep breath, steeling my resolve. "I'm. Not. Dan."

He fought me, but I was ready for him. I tightened my hold on his body and kept going. "Not anymore," I said, rushing to explain as much as I could before I lost control. "Everything's changed. Just give me another chance."

"I can't," she said.

I reached for her, desperate to get her to understand. "Cat, please —"

She flinched when my fingers touched her shoulder, but she didn't pull away. I think she wanted to believe me.

"We can be whatever we like," I said, echoing her phrase from the other night when she'd painted the house. "Please listen to me. The past doesn't matter anymore."

She stepped back. "Why are you doing this to me?"

"You okay?" asked Tricia, inserting herself between us. She glared at me like she thought I'd hurt Cat. The very idea repulsed me, but before I could explain, Dan's thoughts crashed into mine.

Shut up! Shut up! Shut up! I said, or maybe he said it. In that moment, it was hard to tell. I started to lose track of myself.

Dan shut his eyes for several seconds. When he opened them, Tricia had her arm wrapped protectively around Cat, and they were walking away.

The zombie hadn't fully taken control yet. He seemed flustered. I found another gap to slip into.

"Wait!" I called. "I have something for you." I dug into Dan's backpack and pulled out one of the figurines.

"She doesn't want it," Tricia said, steering Cat away.

Fortunately, Cat's backpack was half unzipped. I dropped the Cheshire Cat in, not daring to speak again.

Cat kept walking. I knew she'd find the figurine later. Tomorrow night she'd tell her friends that she wanted a grin without a cat. Perhaps she meant this—a wish fulfilled before she even made it.

My struggle with Dan had exhausted me, so I took shelter in a vestibule to gather my wits. The bell rang, signaling the end of lunch, and everyone headed to their next classes, but I couldn't bring myself to face the rush of people in the hall. I waited until things quieted, then tried to recall Dan's schedule.

Sixth period: biology.

Dan stirred as I approached Mr. Huber's classroom. Cat would be there. Much as I wanted to see her, I was in no shape to fight Dan again. *Focus,* I whispered to myself. *This is your life.* I continued on, deciding not to chance it.

A teacher spotted me and asked why I wasn't in class. I pretended not to hear her and ducked into the portrait hall. My hands shook—whether from hunger or nerves or something else, I couldn't tell. ALARM WILL SOUND IF OPENED stated a sign on the door near the end of the hall. It was the same door Cat would go through tomorrow. I pushed the handle, hoping the alarm had already been broken as I slipped into the overgrown courtyard.

For several minutes, I just stood there, taking in the sunlight and the crisp blue sky. A breeze swirled leaves in a corner. My pulse calmed and Dan withdrew until I was barely conscious of him. It was a relief to escape the claustrophobic pressure of school, where everyone seemed eager to bust you for something. No wonder Cat liked to come out here.

I headed to where she'd sit tomorrow. A few cigarette butts dirtied the ground, but the fallen leaves appeared soft and inviting. The crab-apple tree in front of me had short, stumpy branches and gnarled roots that arched together at the base of the trunk, forming a tiny nook.

The White Rabbit, I thought, realizing this would be the perfect place for him. I dug through Dan's backpack for the remaining figurine.

Tomorrow Cat would come here, thinking she was alone. I imagined her spotting the White Rabbit, his pocket watch clasped in his paw as if he'd been waiting for her to arrive.

She'd probably be surprised at first. She might not even believe it was real. But when she leaned forward and touched the figurine, she'd be filled with wonder.

I figured she'd guess that I'd put it there, yet how I'd known to leave the figurine exactly where she'd see it would be a mystery to her. All she'd know was that I understood her. A connection like that had to resonate, running deeper than words or logic. Deeper than time, even, the way two people could meet each other for the first time and feel like they'd always known each other.

I pressed the figurine into the ground like I was planting a seed. Then I stood, brushed the dirt off the zombie's jeans, and went back inside.

Night

"This is hell," said TR.

He was standing in the middle of the street a little ways from the Coffee Spot, letting cars rush through him, only he wasn't whooping or jumping like he normally did.

"What's wrong?" I asked.

A black sedan blurred through him, but TR kept talking. "I'm not even scared anymore. I don't flinch. Don't get excited. There's nothing left. I think this might be hell."

I sat on the curb, wondering what had changed. The other night, TR had been giddy with the prospect of influencing Waster. "Did something happen today?"

"Nothing happened." TR sat cross-legged in the road as a pickup barreled toward him. "That's the problem. Nothing ever changes. All day I made Waster do things, but it didn't matter."

I chuckled at how wrong he had it.

"What's so funny?" asked TR.

"Let's go inside and I'll tell you about it."

"Tell me what?"

"A secret."

He moved reluctantly, letting the truck plow through half of him. For some reason, that bothered me more than seeing it pass through all of him.

On the way to the diner, I explained the figurines and how I'd given them to Cat. I thought the story might cheer him up, but it only made him more depressed.

"All I did was make Waster call Miss Ashet 'Miss Asshat,'" he said.

"Really? That's great!"

TR frowned.

"I'm serious," I said. "If you can make Waster do that, just think of all the other things you can do."

"What's the point?" He swiped his hand through a lamppost. "We think we're making a difference, but we're not. The same things are still going to happen no matter what we do. We just get to watch. Well, I'm through watching," he said. "I don't want to see it."

"See what?" I asked.

"Any of it. I just want to punch someone, you know? Throw a rock through a window. Do something that makes an impact. I'm sick of living this . . . *ghost* life."

"What if I told you that I know we have an impact," I said. "I know we can make a difference."

TR gave me a skeptical look. "You can't know that."

"But I do," I replied. Then I told him about the messages on the wall and how they'd changed after I'd done things.

His eyes widened.

"That's why you have to take over," I added.

"Take over? Like kick Waster out?" he asked. "Make the corpse my own?"

I nodded.

"You can *do* that?"

I nodded again.

"Holy crap! How?"

I told him about pushing Dan back and walling him off. "It's a battle of wills," I said. "You just need to make your will stronger than his."

"But it's his life."

"Is it?" I asked.

TR cocked his head.

"Waster doesn't have a purpose, right?" I continued.

"He just wanders around all day, going wherever the wind takes him."

"More or less."

"So, if you have a purpose—something bigger than yourself that's important—then you'll be stronger than he is. You'll be able to take over."

"That's it?"

"That, and you need to believe that his life is yours now. You need to make it completely your own."

TR's expression fell. "I don't know, dude. That seems wrong."

"Why? He killed himself, didn't he?"

"Not yet."

I shrugged. "Yesterday. Tomorrow. What's the difference? Waster's pretty much dead already."

"I guess."

"Come on, TR. We'll make their lives ours. We'll fix the things they messed up." I glimpsed Cat through the window of the Coffee Spot, sitting at her usual booth.

"And then what?" asked TR.

"Then who knows?" I said. "We might be released. Or we might start to move forward. That could be our reward for fixing things—we get to live the lives they gave up."

Weekend

Sunday morning, I lay in bed and stared at the ceiling. I figured this was what Dan did most weekends anyway, and the sounds of others in the house comforted me: the bustle of Dan's mom in the kitchen, the murmur of the dishwasher running, Teagan taking a shower and singing to herself.

When Teagan returned to her room, the quiet made me uneasy, so I switched on some music. Dan mostly listened to grating, obnoxious stuff, but there was one song I liked, "The Trapeze Swinger" by Iron and Wine, because it reminded me of Cat. One line, about an angel kissing a sinner, made me wonder if I ever got to kiss her, which one would I be?

Before the song ended, I clicked the button on Dan's iPod to make it play again. The song was almost ten minutes long, but it still seemed too short. I imagined playing it for Cat and asking her to dance. We'd sway together, her chest warm against mine, her head nestled into my neck, both of us wishing the song would never end.

A knock on the door jolted me out of my fantasy. Dan bristled, and I had to concentrate on pushing him back before speaking.

"What is it?" I asked through the door.

"I'm taking a bunch of stuff from the basement to the Goodwill," replied Dan's mom. "If you want to keep anything, now's your chance." Something large thumped in the hallway. "I'll leave this here for you to pick through."

I pulled on pants and a sweatshirt before opening Dan's door. A cardboard box overflowing with clothes, toys, and knickknacks took up half the hallway. Dan protested, but I shut him out. Then I rummaged through the box, finding a man's leather shoe.

The shoe looked used but well cared for—not at all like the zombie's ragged sneakers. It must have belonged to his dad. I slid my foot into it, surprised by how well it fit. My toes sank into worn indents in the insoles. Digging through the box for the other shoe, I spotted the figurines.

The Cheshire Cat and White Rabbit were clumped together in a clear plastic bag, buried beneath naked dolls and stuffed animals. That might explain how they'd gotten into Dan's backpack—I'd put them there. The strange thing was that the bag held a third figurine, a stumpy little man wearing an oversized green top hat and a mustard coat. The Mad Hatter.

Teagan's door swung open. I stuffed the figurines into Dan's back pocket so she wouldn't see them.

"Good morning, Sis," I said.

She glowered at me. Her anger seemed more pronounced than usual, if that was possible. Whatever Dan had done to piss her off must have happened recently.

"Mom's taking this box to the Goodwill," I continued, hoping my cheerful tone would ease the rift between us. "Some of your things are in it if you'd like to keep them."

"I know," said Teagan, squinting. "I helped Mom clean the damn basement."

"Oh. You could have gotten me."

"Why?"

"Because I want to help. I like helping."

She rolled her eyes and retreated to the kitchen.

I considered following her, but Dan had grown increasingly agitated during the conversation, making it difficult to talk.

Once I returned to his room, I searched through his closet for more stuff to give to the Goodwill. Tossing out everything and starting over fresh appealed to me, but Dan would likely object. Instead, I limited myself to getting rid of some of his dullest, dreariest, shabbiest clothes. The guy definitely needed some color in his wardrobe, and it wouldn't kill him to dress up a little more, either. He had several nice shirts that I'd never seen him wear.

A few dusty trophies, baseballs, and other memorabilia cluttered the top shelf of his closet. I got some of them down and read the inscriptions. He'd gotten Varsity Football MVP two years in a row. And he'd been Varsity Baseball Best Hitter the previous year. He also had a shoe box full of medals and ribbons for everything from swimming to track to the eighth-grade science fair. Impressive. Being stuck in his tall, lanky body might not be so bad after all.

Later that day, after showering and cleaning his room, I headed out for a walk. It was overcast, but I liked the way things felt more crisp and defined in the cold. The faint scent of wood smoke and fermenting crab apples tinted the breeze. I ran a few steps. Then sprinted.

Dan resisted. He probably feared looking dumb racing down the block, but he soon gave in. The more I controlled his body, the more solid my hold over him became. This was *my* life. *My* body.

Pretty soon I was jumping bushes and swinging from tree branches, testing out my newly discovered athletic prowess. A whoop of joy escaped my throat. It felt incredible to move like this—lungs burning and muscles flexing. Why Dan didn't run everywhere all the time was beyond me.

A man raking leaves gave me an annoyed look, but I didn't care. I shut my eyes and kept running, taking long, swift strides. Wind whipped my face. I felt like I was flying. I even spread my arms like wings.

Something snagged my foot, clipping my legs out from under me. My eyes snapped open. Time seemed to slow as I watched blades of grass rush past. Each one looked vivid and brilliant. All too soon, I hit the ground and skidded across a lawn, smashing into a couple garden gnomes and taking out a concrete birdbath with my shoulder. An explosion of pain blistered my mind. I recoiled. Immediately, Dan was there, vying for control.

Stupid! I thought. Pain was a trigger for him.

I sank back into him, only it was too late. Dan had already taken over. He gasped for breath and checked his surroundings. A small decorative picket fence marked one end of the yard, about twenty feet back. That must have been what had tripped me. Skid marks streaked the lawn where I'd fallen, and a garden gnome's head had broken off. Dan gave the house a wary look, but no one came out to yell at him. Then he glanced across the street. That's when I realized where we were. Cat's apartment building stood only a block away.

Dan staggered to his feet. The pain from his shoulder had lessened somewhat, but it still hurt. He felt his collarbone and winced. I threw myself into the gap. Dan fought back, but I'd managed to get a foot in the door. We pushed against each other, stumbling about the yard. To anyone watching, we probably looked drunk or insane.

For a moment, I thought he'd win. Then I remembered my purpose. I focused on Cat's apartment and tried to go there.

At last, Dan's hold slipped and I took over, making his body mine again.

I hurried to Cat's front window and hid in the bushes. Her father sat on the couch, his craggy face lit by the flickering glow of the TV. It was the first time I'd seen him in person. Sunday must have been his day off from bartending. Cat was next to him, her back propped against the couch arm as she munched popcorn and watched TV.

Now what? Dan hovered around me, waiting for an opening. If I rang the doorbell, I might not be able to get any words out before he fought me. Besides, I was mud-stained and sweaty from running, and the last time I'd attempted to talk to Cat, it hadn't gone particularly well. I needed a less confrontational way to reach her.

I snuck around the side of her apartment and ducked behind the bushes to reach her bedroom window. Her curtains were open, and her white Christmas lights illuminated her purple walls and *Alice in Wonderland* posters.

The Mad Hatter! It was still in the zombie's back pocket with the two other figurines. I dug it out and arranged it on the window ledge so when Cat looked out her window that night, she'd see the Mad Hatter's wide, cheerful face peering in. It wasn't much, but it was better than nothing, and maybe it would help her feel less alone to know that someone was watching over her.

To know that I was here.

Friday, November 7

I couldn't wait for the weekend to be over so I could go back to school. Even Teagan seemed happy on Friday morning. She didn't scowl or roll her eyes when I greeted her in the kitchen. And after breakfast, she lingered outside Dan's room as if waiting for me.

"Is there something I can do for you?" I asked.

Teagan gave me a confused look. "Aren't we going to school?"

"Together?"

"Uh . . . who else would I get a ride with? Santa Claus and his eight flying reindeer?"

"Right. Very funny," I said, realizing it must have been their usual routine to go together. I grabbed Dan's backpack and headed out through the kitchen. "Bye!" I called to their mom. "We're going to school!"

Dan's mom probably wondered why I sounded like I'd won the lottery, but I didn't care. Things were finally turning around.

I opened the car door for Teagan, then skipped to the driver's side.

"What happened to you?" she asked.

"Nothing. Why?"

"You're acting so *nice.*"

"I like to act nice," I said. "Nice is nice."

Teagan smirked. "What are you? An alien? Did you abduct my brother?"

"No," I said, figuring I should dial things back a bit— be more Dan-like. "I'm just glad it's Friday because we have school. I mean, because it's the *last* day of school this week."

"Tell me about it," said Teagan, getting into Dan's car. "This week sucked."

On the drive, Teagan kept talking about how much her classes "bit," and how Mrs. Byrd, her history teacher, was a "major B," and Mr. Shepherd, the English teacher, was a "nosy-assed slack-hole."

"Definitely," I said, although I liked Mr. Shepherd. He was one of the few teachers who seemed genuinely interested in students' lives. "But he's nice, too," I added.

"Are you serious? The guy thinks he's some sort of teen savior. He made a girl cry the other day because he kept asking her questions about stuff."

"Who?"

"That's not the point," said Teagan. "I thought you hated Mr. Shepherd."

I shrugged. "The important thing is that he cares."

"Whatever. He needs to get a life."

Teagan grew quiet after that, although she kept rubbing her eyes and glancing at me. I tried to come up with something to say that would help her feel appreciated, but everything I thought of sounded either too cheesy for Dan or completely sarcastic coming from him.

"So, I'll meet you by my locker after school?" I asked, pulling into the school parking lot.

"Yeah."

"I hope your day doesn't completely suck."

"Thanks," she said, opening her door. "Same to you."

"Hey, Teagan," I called.

"What?" Her brow furrowed. She was so ready for people to reject her.

"I'm glad that you're my sister."

Teagan's expression softened and she started to smile. Then she caught herself. "Freaking alien," she said.

Heading into school, I was in such a good mood that I completely forgot about Dan's forehead. The wound had been getting worse every day and his hair was slightly shorter, so the scab had become more visible. A few people pointed and stared, until I remembered to pull on a baseball cap like Dan usually did.

I kept an eye out for Cat, but I didn't see her until lunch. She sat at her usual table with Tricia, Teagan, Spooner, and the others. Our eyes met briefly, and then I noticed Finn and some other guys at his table watching. Dan stirred. He'd been fairly quiet all morning, and I didn't want to provoke him now, so I did what he would and retreated to the hallway to eat.

When biology rolled around, I went to class early, eager to see Cat again. She didn't arrive until right before class started, and she didn't look at me. Still, I tried to stay positive. I said hello to people and smiled constantly, figuring it was only a matter of time before attitudes about me shifted. Unfortunately, the nicer I acted, the more people avoided me. It was like they'd gotten so used to Dan being a prick that my sudden friendliness disturbed them.

After class, I went to Dan's locker to get some books. A

guy I'd seen before, hanging around Finn, lingered nearby, as if he wanted to talk to me. He wore a varsity jacket similar to the one Dan had in his locker, so I assumed they were friends.

"Hi, Trent," I said, reading the name off the top of a folder he held. *Trent Mercer.* I remembered Spooner mentioning something about him the other night. "How's it going?"

Trent shrugged. He had dark, wavy hair, a narrow face, and a wide mouth crooked in a perpetual smirk. "I thought you weren't talking to me anymore."

"Why would you think that?"

He scoffed. "Don't be an ass."

I nodded, not sure what to make of this. "That jacket looks good on you," I said to smooth things over.

Trent frowned, like he thought I was being sarcastic.

"It does." I nodded toward Dan's locker where his varsity jacket hung. "I was going to wear mine today. It's cold out."

"You better not," Trent said. "The team wouldn't like that." He peered down the hall for a moment, as if nervous about people catching him with me. "I can't believe you're not playing tonight."

Playing? I thought. Then I remembered the phone conversation Dan would have with his dad a week from now. "Right. Football!" Trent must have played on the team with Dan—that's why they both had varsity jackets. "I quit."

"No kidding." Trent's smirk deepened. "You really screwed things up, you know? You need to make peace with Finn."

"Why?"

"Because he's Finn," he said. "You can't win this, Dan. If people have to choose sides, they're not going to choose yours. You know that. So just say you're sorry and get over it."

My stomach knotted. Dan was growing agitated, thrashing against me. "Okay," I uttered.

Trent checked the hallway again. Students started to file out of the cafeteria. "I better go," he said. "Don't do anything stupid, all right?"

Confused, I watched Trent leave. Here's what I knew: Dan had been on the football team with Trent and Finn. They'd been friends. Dan had even been popular once, according to Cat and Teagan. But then he did something that made everyone—Cat, Teagan, Tricia, even Finn—hate him.

From what I'd observed, Cat liked Finn, and Dan liked Cat, so he might have done something out of jealousy—like when he attacked Finn in Cat's secret house and burned it down. But that wouldn't happen for almost a week. Which meant Dan must have done something else to make everyone turn against him.

I left Dan's varsity jacket in his locker and headed to his next class.

"What up, dude?" called a familiar voice.

I turned. Waster's lopsided, goofy grin greeted me in the hall. It only took me an instant to see that TR had taken control.

"Right on!" I said, relieved to finally see a friendly face. "How's it going?"

"Cool, dude. Very cool," he said. "Chest bump!"

We slammed into each other, and TR started laughing. I laughed, too. It's hard to explain why smashing into each other was so funny, but it was.

"What's wrong with you, man?" asked a guy standing next to Waster. "You know this *pendejo*?"

"Him?" TR winked at me. "Of course not. I don't know him at all."

"Later," I said, not wanting to ruin TR's cover.

"That's right—you better get out of my way." TR tried to sound tough, but I could hear his laughing voice beneath Waster's rough grumble.

I waved to him and continued walking while Waster's friend made some comment about preppy-ass jock-wads like me.

★   ★   ★

Teagan came by Dan's locker after school.

"Ready to go?" I asked, glad she'd decided to meet me there. I didn't have a clue where her locker might be.

She shook her head. Her face looked paler than usual, and her eyes were red, as if she'd been crying.

"What happened?" I asked.

"I need to talk to you," she said. "Outside."

"Sure. Let me get my books."

I fiddled with Dan's lock, but I had trouble remembering his combo. Besides, I didn't know what books to grab since I hadn't paid attention in class. Note for next time — remember what homework would get collected.

Teagan was already halfway out the door when I gave up on the locker and jogged after her. Something definitely seemed wrong, but thinking this roused Dan. I took a few deep breaths and focused on walling him off. Then I threw open the door and stepped out.

Teagan paced by the flagpole. Her expression appeared more angry than sad.

"Is it true?" she asked.

"Is what true?"

She waited until a group of students passed before continuing. "What you did to Cat Slater."

Dan slammed against me. I stepped back, struggling to compose myself. He'd never rebelled so abruptly before. It was unnerving. "I'm . . . not . . . sure what you're talking about," I said.

"Bullshit. You know exactly what I'm talking about. That's why you're sweating."

She was right—I *was* sweating. I was shaking, too. "What did you hear?"

"The whole school thinks you two hooked up. . . ." Her voice dwindled. "It was at that party, wasn't it?"

"What party?"

"Stop treating me like I'm stupid. The Halloween party."

"Oh. *That* party." I nodded, pretending I understood while Dan raged around me, looking for a gap. I had to stay calm. Do what he'd do.

"That's it? You're not going to deny it?" she asked.

"Deny what?"

"I can't believe this. I stuck up for you," said Teagan.

"Whatever I did, I'll fix it," I said. "I'll make it better."

"Make it better?" Her voice grew so taut she could barely speak. "What you did to Cat is the worst thing. You can't make it better. Not this."

"Not what?"

Teagan's brow knotted. "Tricia said . . ." She stopped, obviously not wanting to say what she'd heard.

"Go on."

"She said you . . . *raped* Cat."

The word made no sense to me at first, but it lodged in my mind with barbed hooks. I pictured the lewd drawing on the library sign-in sheet of Dan and Cat together. Everyone thought Dan and Cat had hooked up, but they didn't know the truth. They didn't know he'd forced her. Except for Tricia. That's why she hated Dan. And that's why Cat said she didn't want to see him ever again.

Teagan waited for me to deny it. I think she wanted me to say it was all a lie or a vicious rumor so I could go back to being her brother. But I couldn't. I felt too sick to say anything.

My silence was all the confirmation Teagan needed. Her face crumpled and she stormed off.

I slumped against the wall. I was in love with Cat and trapped in the body of her rapist.

TR was right. This was hell.

Night

I tore out of the zombie the moment he lost consciousness. All I could think about was getting as far from Dan as possible. Before long, I found myself near Cat's place. TR sat on the curb in front of her apartment, waiting for me. I hid behind some bushes across the street, not sure what I'd say to him. That's when I noticed Cat's window.

Her curtains were pulled open, which surprised me. Usually she kept them closed. Unless she only started closing them *after* she discovered the Mad Hatter on her windowsill.

Oh, God, I whispered, realizing what I'd done. Cat would think the figurines came from Dan. Each one would be a reminder of how he'd attacked her—a sign that she couldn't escape him, no matter where she went. She wouldn't feel safe in her room anymore or in the courtyard at school—not after discovering the White Rabbit there. That's why Tricia accused Dan of harassing Cat. Only Dan wasn't responsible for harassing her. I was.

There had to be a way to change what I'd done. But how? My past was set, even if it was her future.

I left before TR saw me and headed away from town. Most of the streets looked empty, but cars raced through the night on the highway. Their lights grew brighter, turning from white to red as they passed. I stepped into the far lane and watched a semi approach. Every instinct in me screamed to get out of the way. Closing my eyes, I waited for the impact.

The truck rushed through me, quick as a breeze. Then another. And another.

Nothing happened.

I stayed in the road for hours. At first, I wanted to punish myself for making things worse for Cat. But the more cars tore through me, the more I realized they wouldn't hurt—not the way I wanted them to. It was like jumping from the top of the radio tower and *not* falling.

I cursed at the oncoming cars. I even ran toward the

rushing metal, attempting to add the force of my will to the impact. It made little difference.

Finally, I gave up and lay in the road. I let the black tires pass through my head, wishing I could escape it all, but it was a child's fantasy—simple as thinking that shutting your eyes will keep others from seeing you.

When the sky began to lighten, I walked away from town, putting as much distance between myself and Dan as I could. The sun rose, and I walked faster. Maybe if I got far enough away, I wouldn't be called back.

No such luck. In some distant room, I heard Dan's alarm go off. Then the reeling came, ripping me inside out until I slammed to a sickening halt in the body of the last person on earth I wanted to be.

Thursday, November 6

My new mission was to keep Dan as far from Cat as possible. In fact, I needed to keep him away from Teagan and his mom and anyone else he might hurt, too. The less he was around, the better—that much seemed certain. And if I hadn't already come to this conclusion on my own, the message I found carved into the wall that morning would have made it abundantly clear:

WHATEVER YOU DO WILL MAKE THINGS WORSE

No duh, I thought, wanting to punch the wall. Then again, that might only "make things worse."

As far as clues went, the messages sucked. Instead of proclaiming YOU ARE NOT WHO YOU THINK YOU ARE, why didn't the last message just tell me that Dan was a rapist? Then I wouldn't have been an idiot about trying to be with Cat. A fortune cookie would have been more helpful.

Once I took a shower and calmed down some, I thought about the new message again. Given that whatever I did, or Dan did, would make things worse, the best course of action seemed to not "do" anything.

Which is easier said than done.

After shaving, I rummaged through the medicine cabinet and swallowed several allergy pills with a "May Cause Drowsiness" warning on them. For good measure, I washed the pills down with a hearty swig of cold medicine. I worried a little about Dan taking over if I got sleepy, but it didn't work like that. The drugs mostly affected the body, not me. With any luck, we'd pass out before school, and then I wouldn't have to worry about Dan hurting anyone.

Unfortunately, the main thing the medicine did was give me a vicious case of heartburn. Then, on the drive to school, my vision began to blur. I considered swerving into a tree — that would take Dan out of the picture for a while. Too bad Teagan was in the car with me. I couldn't risk injuring her. In her time zone, Dan was still the big brother she looked up to.

While I drove, Teagan talked up a storm, filling me in on trivial things that had happened recently. When we arrived at school, she hesitated before getting out.

"Good luck today," she said, giving me a look like I was going off to war. "Don't let the pricks get you down."

"Welcome back," said Mr. Walker, Dan's homeroom teacher.

"Thanks," I replied, wondering what the occasion might be. It was the first time Mr. Walker had ever greeted me like that. "Did I go somewhere fun?"

Mr. Walker's expression darkened. "Let's hope not," he said. "Being suspended isn't meant to be a vacation. Nor is it a legitimate excuse for turning in late work."

Suspended, I thought. *That'll work*. At least being suspended would give me a way to avoid people for the next few days.

I grew dizzy as the morning progressed, but the drugs didn't fully kick in until second period, when Mr. Shepherd started to sound like he was lecturing through the far end of a garden hose.

At the end of the period, Mr. Shepherd called me up to his desk. A thin stream of drool trickled down my chin.

I wiped my mouth on my sleeve and touched my cheeks to make sure Dan's face was still there. For the last half hour, I'd felt like a wax sculpture standing too close to a fire. Fortunately, the dulled senses made it easy to keep Dan disconnected.

Mr. Shepherd scanned his grade book while I stood before his desk. He had a receding hairline that made his widow's peak resemble a uvula, which, as I'd learned in biology, was the thing that dangles in the back of one's throat. The image struck me as oddly humorous, and before I knew it, I snorted with laughter.

"Something funny?" asked Mr. Shepherd.

"No," I said, not wanting to offend him.

Mr. Shepherd gave me a stern look. I realized I was still grinning.

"Am I in trouble?" I asked, attempting to compose a more appropriate expression. Maybe the drugs *had* affected me some.

"I'm not sure. Are you?" asked Mr. Shepherd.

The zombie's eyes wavered in and out of focus. Was I in trouble? Definitely. But if I told Mr. Shepherd about my situation, he'd think I was crazy. "I don't believe I did anything wrong in class," I said.

"No. You didn't," agreed Mr. Shepherd. "In fact, you haven't done anything in class in a while." His forehead wrinkled as he scanned his grade book. "You haven't participated in discussion lately, you ruined your perfect quiz score, and you missed the last four homework assignments."

"I didn't remember them," I said, which was factually true. How could I remember what hadn't happened yet?

"I'm worried about you, Dan," said Mr. Shepherd. "What's going on?"

I glanced at the door, wishing I could get out of there, but if I left now, it might, as the ever-so-helpful drywall oracle put it, "make things worse." Besides, I felt bad for Mr. Shepherd. He was just trying to help. "Listen," I said. "I really appreciate your concern, but I'm fine. There's nothing you can do."

Mr. Shepherd looked perturbed. "Is that so?"

"Yeah," I said. "Some things went wrong, but I'm working on it. I'm going to fix it."

"You used to be a model student, and now your grades are slipping. You got suspended. You've been fighting with your friends."

"I have?" This was news to me. "Which friends?"

Mr. Shepherd breathed a frustrated sigh. "I may only be a teacher, but I still see things," he said. "You don't seem *fine* to me." He leaned back in his chair and crossed his arms. "Is it a girl?"

"What?"

"The reason you're upset. Is it a girl?"

I glanced at the door again. It didn't help that my face felt like it was sliding off and my lips tingled. "You could say that."

Mr. Shepherd nodded. "Things might seem serious now. You might think you're in love and you'll never love anyone again. But believe me, a lot is going to change in your life. Someday you'll look back on all this high-school drama and laugh about it."

No, I thought. *I won't laugh about it, and neither will Dan. He'll slash his wrists and bleed to death in a tub.*

"Just keep things in perspective," continued Mr. Shepherd. "High school doesn't last forever."

That's for sure, I thought, only I couldn't say this. "Thanks, Mr. Shepherd," I told him, slurring the words slightly. "I'll keep that in mind."

Lunch claimed it was sloppy joes, but the ice-cream scoop of meat on a bun that was plopped on my plate looked and smelled suspiciously like dog food. I wasn't in much of a mood to eat anyway. My limbs wobbled from all the medicine, and my thoughts kept getting caught in the tar pit of Mr. Shepherd's kindness. He wouldn't have been so nice to me if he'd known what Dan had done.

"Danny!"

My senses reeled as Dan lunged to take control. I tried

to force him back, but something about the guy's voice put the zombie in a frenzy. Whispers swirled around me. I turned — whether by my own will or Dan's I wasn't sure.

"Wake up," said Finn.

Trent Mercer stood beside him, looking twitchy.

I focused on maintaining control. Dan was furious, but there was no way I'd let him take over. For a moment we fought against each other, pushing on either side of a door. Then the door clicked shut, and I was able to reconnect. "What do you want?" I asked.

"Coach wants to see you," said Finn.

"Now?" My voice wavered as Dan pounded the door.

"No," joked Trent. "In ten years at the next reunion. Don't be such a zombie."

I froze. "What did you call me?"

"Relax, man," said Trent. "I'm just saying you look like a zombie with that scab on your forehead, drooling and stumbling around like you're asleep." He stuck his arms out and made his face go slack, doing a crude imitation of me.

Dan filled my head with angry whispers. "Shut up!" I snapped.

Trent's expression fell. So much for being nice to people. I had to get away before Dan took over.

"Better hurry," said Finn. "Coach is waiting." If he

was mad at me, he didn't sound it. Instead, he seemed concerned.

"Right." I started for the door, forgetting that I still had a lunch tray in my hands. Milk tipped, spilling onto my plate and shirt. A few people chuckled.

"You all right?" Finn asked, moving closer. All around me, I could feel students watching us. Finn kept his voice low. "Be careful what you say, okay? I wouldn't want you to get in any more trouble."

I looked at Finn. He held my gaze, and his face broke into an easy, encouraging smile.

"Thanks," I told him. I set the tray on top of a trash can and hurried out before Dan could mess things up.

Coach's office occupied the back corner of the boys' locker room. A large window took up most of one wall, revealing Coach, bent over his desk, writing in a binder. I paused outside his door to collect myself.

"Come in," he said without looking up. He taught civics class as well, but everyone, even the other teachers, called him Coach. "Take a seat."

I slumped in the chair across from him. Coach chewed his gum and studied me for several seconds. Maybe he was waiting for me to start the conversation, but I had no clue why I'd been called here.

Coach opened his desk drawer, took out his gum, and put it on a piece of tinfoil. "Damn nicotine gum tastes like cardboard," he said.

My face must have reflected my confusion.

"You didn't know I smoked?" Coach asked.

"No."

"I've been trying to quit for twenty years. The gum helps me make it through the day."

I nodded, sensing he was letting me in on something personal.

"So," he said, "give me one reason why I should keep you on the team."

"I don't have a reason."

"Are you quitting?"

I shrugged.

"Not good enough," said Coach. "If you're quitting, at least have the courtesy to tell me why."

I considered telling Coach that Dan had raped the girl I loved, only there was no way I'd get the words out. Even thinking this caused Dan to push against me. Besides, what would happen to Cat if I blabbed about what Dan had done? There might be an investigation. She might be forced to talk about things she didn't want to talk about.

"No reason," I muttered, staring at the floor. "I just don't think I'm good for the team."

"Why don't you let me decide what's good for the

team?" replied Coach. "Principal Murphy thinks you should be suspended from play for the rest of the season. I went out on a limb to get him to consider making an exception for you. So what do you say, Dan?" Coach thumped his hands against the desktop and leaned forward. "Should I give you a second chance?"

My eyes flicked back to his. I hadn't meant to look at Coach, but now that I had, I couldn't turn away. Wrinkles branched from the corners of his eyes like river deltas. Something about him reminded me of a picture of Dan's dad that I'd found in his room. They didn't really look alike, but the way he gazed at me made me want to not let him down.

"Do you ever wish you could start over?" I asked.

"I wish I'd never started smoking," Coach said. "We all screw up, Dan. The important thing is to learn from our mistakes and move on."

"Yeah, but what if you can't move on?" I asked. "What if your mistakes are too big?"

Coach sighed. "Sometimes I think you're too hard on yourself, Dan. You can't take responsibility for everything that goes wrong."

"Even if you are responsible?" I asked.

"Is there something you want to tell me?"

I shook my head. "I'm just thinking."

"Everyone drops the ball sometimes," said Coach.

"You just need to get back in the game and do your best. What doesn't kill us makes us stronger, right? So if you make a big mistake, then you learn a big lesson."

"You do?"

"Sure you do," said Coach. "Even if it means chewing crappy gum for years." He shifted his jaw. "So, will I see you at practice today? You owe me some laps."

I imagined what it would be like for Cat if Dan became a big varsity football star again. She'd have to go to Friday pep rallies and watch students cheer him on. And while he scored touchdowns, she'd get called a slut.

"I don't think so, Coach."

"You don't *think* so?"

"No," I said. "I won't be coming back."

Teagan was waiting for me at the zombie's locker after school. I figured she'd be there. This was the encounter I'd dreaded most. Out of all the people Dan knew, she'd be the hardest to push away.

She called Dan's name, but I kept walking, pretending I hadn't seen her.

"I need to tell you something," she said.

I slowed and looked at the ground, like Dan would. "What?" I muttered, going for an annoyed tone.

Teagan glanced around, clearly wanting to speak to

me in private, but I didn't budge. *This is for the best,* I told myself.

"There's a text going around," she said. "My friend Laney got it three times. Someone even sent it to me."

"So?"

"So it's a list of guys to avoid," said Teagan. "And your name's on it."

Good, I thought. *It should be on it.*

"I erased your name before sending it on," Teagan continued. "I even had Laney erase it."

"You shouldn't have done that."

"Why not? People are just being a-holes because you punched Finn," she said. "He's probably the one who sent the text. Or Kendra. She practically worships Finn. I'm glad you hit him."

Dan hit Finn? When I'd seen Finn at lunch, he hadn't mentioned anything about that.

"I could send out a text saying the other text is a lie," she said.

"No."

"You can't let them smear you like this."

It killed me how certain of Dan's innocence she was, but everything she did to defend him today would only come back to haunt her tomorrow. "Leave it alone, Teagan."

"I'm trying to help you."

"Well, don't. I don't want your help."

"What's your problem?"

"You," I said. "You're my problem. Stop messing with my life."

Teagan flinched and her chin trembled. I hated treating her like that, but I had to do it. I had to make her dislike me. And the disturbing thing was, I was pretty good at it, too.

Night

"Where were you last night?" asked TR as soon as I slipped out of the zombie's room. "I waited for you at the Coffee Spot for almost an hour, then I went to Cat's house and watched her do this whole striptease routine. Dude, you should have seen it."

"You better not—"

"Kidding," he said. "When I didn't find you at Cat's, I went back to the Coffee Spot and listened to this guy tell some girl about how he had three near-death experiences and he didn't see diddly-squat, so he doesn't believe in spirits or angels or anything. Wish I could have jabbed him with a fork."

TR set off for Cat's neighborhood, assuming that's where I wanted to go. "So where were you?" he asked again.

"I had trouble getting out," I lied.

"Your corpse pull an all-nighter or something?"

"Something like that," I said. "I didn't see you in school today."

"I wasn't there," TR answered. "Waster had a funeral to go to."

As we walked, he told me more about his day. Apparently, the funeral was for a kid, just four years old. Waster's cousin or second cousin — TR wasn't sure which. His name was Mateo, and he'd wandered out onto a busy road on Saturday when no one was watching and got hit by a car. The worst part was that the car kept going, so no one was even with him when he died.

"It sucked," said TR. "I would have given anything not to have to go to that funeral, but Waster's mom made me. So I put on a suit that fit too tight and rode in the backseat to the service, trying to play the part. But when I got there, I couldn't even step into the room where the service was. Waster kept churning inside, making me sick. I finally had to back off, but he didn't try to take over."

"Weird."

"I think he wanted to disappear," said TR. "Some people seemed to be whispering about him, only no one would talk to him. The whole time, I stayed outside the service doors, looking in. And all I could think about was that poor kid, curled up on the side of the road like a stray dog, dying alone. It's not fair, you know? Cars go right through us, so why not him? If I could trade places with him for a second . . ." TR's voice broke off.

"You okay?" I asked.

"Sure, why wouldn't I be?" he said. "You know they make caskets for kids? The 'American Baby' retails for four hundred and ninety dollars plus shipping and is hand assembled from oak in southern India. It comes lined with yellow or blue satin, fully padded. Or, if you're on a budget, there's the 'Infant Tribute' model, which comes unpadded for only two hundred and ninety-nine dollars, but you need to know the length and weight of your child before ordering."

I gave him a perplexed look.

"I spent an hour flipping through the casket catalog," he said.

We turned onto Cat's street. I got the sense that TR had more than casket prices on his mind, but I didn't want to press him on it. I had my own problems to worry about.

"After the service, I wanted to get out of there," he continued. "I mean *out*. So I walked home, and when I got back, I dug through Waster's drawers and found a bottle of vodka. I made him drink until he passed out."

"Uh-huh," I said. Cat's curtains were open again. Just like I'd feared—she'd only start closing them *after* I left the Mad Hatter there.

"You want to go jump off a building?" I asked. "Or we could lie on the train tracks for a while. Watch the cars pass overhead."

"Naw, man," said TR. "We got to find the lever that will fix things. Right?"

"Right," I agreed. Except I didn't want TR to find out what Dan had done. It's not that I cared about protecting Dan. I hated him more than ever now, but like it or not, I inhabited the zombie. I'd made his life mine, and I couldn't stand the thought of TR looking at me like *I* was a rapist.

TR paused outside Cat's room. "Ladies first," he said.

I glanced around the apartment courtyard, trying to think of somewhere else we could go.

"Or not," he muttered.

"Wait!" I called, but TR was already halfway through the wall.

I hurried after him. It took me a few seconds to adjust before I could make out Cat asleep in bed. Her clock said it was a quarter after eleven. Her arm stretched across her pillow, and the blankets had slid off her shoulder. I wanted to tuck her in.

TR drifted around her room, but he didn't point out

anything of interest. "They even make caskets out of cardboard," he said. "The one in the funeral service was a fancy model. Carved lid. Dark walnut with blue velvet interior. I saw it when people came out. It was the size of a toy chest, and the lid was open." He paused. "I didn't want to look, you know? But I had to. The kid inside, he was so small and alone."

"That sounds rough," I said.

TR shrugged. "If we go backwards a couple more days, he'll be alive again."

"Sure."

"But that doesn't change anything," continued TR. "I'll still know what's going to happen to him. I'll still see his mom and grandparents crying and tearing out their hair. And I'll still see Mateo in that casket."

I slumped back onto Cat's bed. Most of the time TR just rambled on and made jokes, but every now and then he said something that cut straight to the bone.

Cat stirred next to me. I studied her sleeping face. TR was right—and not just about the kid. If I didn't stop the rape from happening, I'd always know it was going to happen to her. I'd never be able to look at her without thinking of what was coming. Without knowing I hadn't saved her when I could.

Suspension

Dan's mom pounded on his door. I'd planned on sleeping in, since Dan was suspended, but she obviously had other ideas.

"I'm awake!" I shouted.

"This is a punishment, not a break," she called back. "Make sure you do your homework and clean your room. Don't watch TV all day."

"I won't."

Keys rattled. After an awkward pause, her footsteps receded and the garage door rumbled open.

According to Dan's cell phone, it was Wednesday, November 5. If the party Teagan had mentioned occurred on Halloween night, then I had five more days before the past was set. Five days to fix things.

I checked the message written beneath the calendar. It still said WHATEVER YOU DO WILL MAKE THINGS WORSE. The problem was, I couldn't be sure who the "you" referred to—Dan or me? Dan had definitely made things worse for Cat. But I'd made things worse by stalking Cat and leaving her the figurines. Either way, it seemed best to keep avoiding people. Being suspended might actually help.

I hid in Dan's room until Teagan and his mom were gone. Then I passed most of the day on the couch, watching game shows and eating cereal. When Teagan got home, I locked myself in the zombie's bedroom and put on his headphones. If she knocked on the door, I didn't hear it. Boring as it was to stay isolated like that, at least it kept Dan from getting agitated and taking over.

Tuesday started out pretty much the same, only the thought of being stuck inside for another day made me want to scream. To make things tolerable, I downed a bunch of medicine like I had before. This time the package of allergy pills was unopened and the cough syrup bottle looked full. Dan resisted swallowing the pills, but I shut him out and took one. Then two. Then some more, until I was popping them like M&M's and washing them down with cough syrup during *Wheel of Fortune*. I figured whatever the pills did had to be an improvement. Things turned out better than I'd anticipated, though, when a few minutes into *Jeopardy!* Dan passed out on the couch.

I gradually loosened my hold on his body. Even if Dan took over now, what could he do? The drugs wouldn't leave his system anytime soon. I backed away, straining against the bonds that kept me there. It wasn't as easy as at night, when slipping out had become second nature, but I managed to break free.

For a moment, I hovered above him. Dan lay against the end of the couch, drooling. A few crumbs from breakfast dotted his T-shirt, and his head slumped uncomfortably against a cushion. The thought of getting reeled in made me anxious. Given all the pills I'd taken, though, I figured he'd be unconscious for a while.

I left the house and crossed the yard, thrilled to be out during the day for a change. Maybe it was only a trick of perception, but I actually felt warmed by the sun.

All around me, the world pulsed with movement and sound—cars rushed past on the street; an elderly man walked his dog; a cat prowled the bushes, sending a pair of doves flapping into the sky. I hurried to school. The closer I got, the more the air hummed with activity. Gym class must have been taking place, because Coach blew his whistle and shouted at a group of guys walking the track. I'd neglected to check the clock before leaving, but given that several students were hanging around, eating chips and kicking a Hacky Sack, it must have been close to noon.

I passed through the front doors and coasted down halls teeming with students. In the anonymous herd, I felt surprisingly present. I'd never realized how exhausting inhabiting a body could be, but now I didn't have to worry about how people saw me or what I should do.

I spotted Trent talking to a few guys by his locker and drifted closer. Normally, I got edgy around him since I never knew how Dan might react, but without a body all that anxiety fell away. There was nothing to do but watch. Almost immediately, I noticed things I never had before. The nervous bob of his head when he spoke. The way his smirk twitched at the corners of his mouth. How he kept glancing around, even while talking to someone, as if looking for someone else.

A sophomore wearing a scarf walked past and brushed his fingers across the small of Trent's back. Trent didn't turn, but his smile tightened and he laughed too loud at something someone said. The sophomore ducked into the boys' bathroom. A few minutes later, the bell rang and students cleared out of the hall, darting into their classes. Trent waited until almost everyone had gone, then he slipped into the bathroom. I followed, caught in his current.

"Hey, fag," he said, once the door had shut behind him. "What was that?"

"No one saw," replied the sophomore. I'd noticed him hanging out with the jazz-band kids before, but I didn't know his name. I think he played guitar. "No one's here."

Trent stepped closer. I expected him to throw the sophomore against the wall or say something threatening, only the moment they touched, everything changed. They spilled into a stall, kissing.

Every time I'd seen Trent before, he'd been partially obscured, but now he came into focus. *This* was why he made obnoxious comments and teased people. He constantly feared being himself. An exquisite rush of understanding filled me.

I drifted through walls into classrooms, eager to see more. The people I looked at shimmered like artifacts on museum shelves, with all their facets and details illuminated. A girl in Dan's math class who often raised her hand when the teacher asked a question crumpled up a test and pressed a compass point against her thigh because she'd missed one problem. A boy in the music practice room who'd never once spoken a word in Dan's English class played a drum set with wild abandon. A senior who looked like a marine snuck out of class to write a poem in marker on the inside of someone's locker, while a few doors down a teacher watched and didn't say a word.

Everyone concealed a secret self that almost no one else knew.

During the time between classes, eyeglasses got crushed beneath feet. Notes were exchanged. Drugs changed hands. Some people were shoved or kicked. Others hugged. Some said yes. Others, no. So much could happen in a minute, in a second even — moments of kindness and cruelty, declarations of love and loneliness, possibilities found and lost — while people walked by, fumbling in their own self-conscious worlds.

In the cafeteria, I spotted Cat at the salad bar, surrounded by Kendra, Bella, and Laney. "Did you have a nice weekend, slut?" Kendra asked. "What made you think you could go to that party, anyway?"

Bella said something, too, but I didn't hear it because Cat was walking away. She hurried out of the cafeteria, struggling to keep a brave face.

Tricia caught up to her in the hallway. "You all right?" she asked.

Cat nodded, but her eyes were wet and her voice shook. "I'm great," she said. "Blue skies."

"What did they say to you?" asked Tricia.

"Does it matter?"

"If they said something about what happened, God help me, I'll beat the crap out of them. Literally."

"Let it go, Tricia."

"I'm not going to let it go. Not this. They can't throw this in your face." She scowled at the cafeteria doors. "Kendra told Laney you tried to sleep with the whole team."

Cat glared at her. "Why are you telling me this?"

"Because people need to know the truth."

"What truth? That I was drunk and stupid?"

"You weren't just drunk," said Tricia. "Trust me. One drink wouldn't make you pass out."

"It doesn't matter." Cat leaned against the lockers and slid down until she was sitting. "I'm not even sure what happened."

"Bullshit," said Tricia. "You *know* what happened."

"You weren't there. You didn't see me," said Cat. "A lot of people are telling the same story."

"So? People are always telling stories."

"What if it's true? There are pictures of me online. Everyone's seen them. I can tell by the way they look at me. Everyone thinks I'm a slut."

"You're not." Tricia sat next to Cat. "I know you. And I know what you told me. You can't let Dan get away with this."

Cat hugged her knees.

"If you don't tell someone, he'll do it again," added Tricia.

"So it will be my fault?"

"Of course not. It's not your fault at all."

Cat scoffed. "Did you read that in a pamphlet somewhere?"

"What are you getting mad at me for?"

"Because I'm sick of you playing psychologist," said Cat. "All you do is follow me around. Live through me. I don't want to be part of your freak show anymore."

Tricia's face reddened. "Cat, you need to deal with this."

"There's *nothing* to deal with," Cat said, standing. "I'm not going to talk about this ever again."

After the last bell rang, I watched Cat leave school. She walked home alone. I didn't see Tricia anywhere. A car slowed alongside Cat as she approached the end of the parking lot. The passenger window rolled down, then a guy yelled, "Hey, Cat-Lip! What about me? I play football."

Cat looked over, stony-faced and dazed. Someone tossed a soda at her and laughed.

Dozens of people in the parking lot saw, but no one did anything. Most people just looked away. Others sneered or smirked.

Cat wiped her face on her sleeve and continued walking, eyes locked on the concrete in front of her. She didn't slow down until she was a couple blocks away. Then she tried to wipe more of the soda off her face, but it had mostly dried, leaving a sticky brown mess.

I followed her home. Her father was in the kitchen, getting ready for another long night at the bar. "I made waffles," he said. Tattoos of children's book characters decorated his arms—the dancing monsters from *Where the Wild Things Are*, Eeyore and Piglet from *Winnie-the-Pooh*, and Alice falling in a blue dress.

Cat looked at the waffle her dad set on the counter. It had two halves of a strawberry arranged for eyes and a whipped-cream smile.

Her blank expression started to crack. She ducked into her room and locked the door.

Cat's dad asked what was wrong. She tried to tell him she wasn't hungry, but she couldn't get her voice to sound normal. He lingered in the hallway, fiddling with the cigarettes in his pocket. "I have to go to work," he said through the door. "There are eggs for dinner if you don't want the waffle."

Once he was gone, she opened her soda-splattered backpack, pulled out her notebook, and turned to a blank page. At the top, she wrote two words: *The Party.*

After that, she didn't write a thing. She just stared at the blank page like she wanted to remember more, but she couldn't. Then she tore the page out and lit a candle—the same candle she'd use to burn the pictures of herself, only now it was taller. She opened her window and held the corner of the page over the flame until the paper caught.

When the flames were halfway up the page, she seemed to realize she had no place to drop it. She turned her hand so the flames curled away from her. Still the fire inched toward her fingers. She winced and clenched her teeth, but she didn't let go.

Flames licked her fingers, singeing her nails and skin.

Let it go, I urged.

She didn't. Perhaps she couldn't. Not really. How do you let go of something you can't remember?

At last, she shook the page away from her hand. There was only a tiny triangle of paper left where her fingers had been. It burned in the air, leaving a gray skein of ashes that broke apart and scattered into thousands of pieces, so light they barely even fell.

Night

As soon as I returned to Dan's house, I checked the message on the wall, but it hadn't changed. WHATEVER YOU DO WILL MAKE THINGS WORSE.

The drugs wore off, leaving me jittery and out of sorts for the rest of the day. Unfortunately, I couldn't get Dan's body to fall asleep until late, probably because of the four-hour nap he'd taken. By the time I finally managed to slip out again, it was almost two in the morning.

I found TR lying on a picnic table in the courtyard of Cat's apartment complex, staring at the stars.

"You been inside?" I asked.

He nodded, but he didn't say anything.

I passed through Cat's walls into her room, fearing what I'd find. She lay in bed, trying to sleep, but her hand seemed to be bothering her. She had an icepack by her pillow and she kept pressing her fingers against it and cringing. I hated that I hadn't been able to help her. When I slipped free of Dan, I was powerless. And when I was in him, I was the last person Cat would ever want to see.

Whatever you do will make things worse, I muttered. Such a pointless, paradoxical message. Trying to do nothing was the same as doing something. There was no way *not* to make things worse. So what the hell was I supposed to do?

TR stepped in a few minutes later. "When you didn't show up at the C Spot, I came here to look for you," he said. "She was asleep by then. I think she burned her hand." TR must have seen that I was upset, because he added, "Don't blame yourself, dude. There was nothing you could do."

"You're right," I said. "*I'd* only make things worse."

"I didn't say that," replied TR.

"There was nothing *I* could do," I repeated, suddenly getting the message.

"It's just, you know, shit happens," TR continued. "You can't fix everything." He rambled on, trying to make me feel better, but I was too caught up in my thoughts to respond.

193

If the message was right, and everything I did, or Dan did, would make things worse, then there was only one solution. Someone else had to do something for Cat.

But who?

Monday, November 3

TO FIX THIS, YOU MUST DIE

I read the message several times. Outside, the sun was shining. Birds were chirping. The world seemed full of possibilities, while I contemplated death threats from a wall. Hell of a way to start the day.

Then again, at least the message was different. The way I saw it, the messages were like keys to doors. I didn't know which key was right until the door opened. And then the message would switch. So the fact that there was a new message meant I'd changed something. I'd opened a door.

Of course, I still didn't know who the "you" referred to—Dan or me? Dan was going to die in twelve days, anyway. Was that what the message meant, or did Dan need to die sooner, before he hurt Cat? And if I got him to kill himself, would I even exist?

Some things you can't think your way out of. Not ever. I tried to assure myself that when the time was right, the message would become clear. Until then, there was no point stressing about it.

I wolfed down some breakfast, grabbed Dan's varsity jacket from his room, and headed for the garage before Teagan could ask for a ride. I didn't want to deal with her on top of everything else.

The chill morning air slapped me awake. Frost glistened on the lawn and lined the edges of leaves. Good thing Dan's jacket had been hanging in his room instead of collecting dust in his locker. The heavy cloth and padded sleeves comforted me as I drove to school and shuffled to the front doors. I expected the usual silent treatment from the students gathered there, but the moment I arrived on campus, I was the center of attention.

"Hey, stud, have fun at the party?" asked one guy in a *wink-wink* way that made me want to simultaneously punch him and puke on my shoes.

All morning, guys asked me similar questions, grinning stupidly like they couldn't wait to hear my answer.

Was this who Dan hung out with? If so, I could understand why he killed himself. I tried to ignore the guys, but the quieter I got, the more they pressed me for details while Dan grew increasingly irritated. And of course people asked about the wound on my forehead.

"I ran into a wall," I told Dave, this guy in Dan's second-period English class. I still had no clue what had really happened, but I figured if I came up with a boring answer, people would lose interest and stop asking. Big mistake.

"A *wall*?" repeated Dave. "Were you drunk?"

"Did you fly into it, Superman?" teased another guy.

"Naw. He probably crashed through it, like the Hulk," joked his friend.

"Seriously, what happened?" asked Dave.

"I already told you, I ran into a wall," I said, but none of them bought it.

The rumors spread quickly after that. For the rest of the day, people questioned me about getting my butt kicked by a gang or smacked by a tree branch or jumped by a ninja. I was more popular now than ever, and I hated it. Unfortunately, the more I downplayed things, the more people thought I must be hiding something juicy.

At lunch, Trent and Finn and a couple other guys at their table nodded to me, as if they expected me to sit with them. A few wore varsity jackets. Fellow football thugs. I approached the table, worried that Trent might say something about the jacket I wore, but he didn't. Everyone acted friendly.

"Hey, Danny boy," said Dave, the guy who'd given me crap about my head wound earlier. "We were just talking about you."

"You were?" Dan churned. I had to stay calm. In control.

"It's all good," said Finn. He scooted over to make room for me. "Aren't you going to sit?"

I set my tray down next to Finn's, ignoring the rising tempest of Dan's thoughts. If I walked away, it might make things worse.

"You looked like you were heading someplace else," said Finn.

"No. I was just looking for someone." The excuse wasn't a complete lie—I'd been looking for Cat all morning, although I was fairly certain she'd skipped school today.

Finn raised an eyebrow. "Who?"

"His girlfriend," interjected Dave. "Cat-Lip."

"She's not my girlfriend," I said, a little too sharply. A few other guys looked over.

"Just a one-night stand, then?" teased Dave. "You heartbreaker. Is she the one who hit you?"

"Don't be an ass," said Finn.

"What?" exclaimed Dave. "I just want to know if she was rough. I hear freaky chicks are rough."

"I heard she was trashed," said this guy with hair so blond it looked white. "You see those pictures of her online?"

"What pictures?" asked another guy.

I thought of the pictures Cat would mention tomorrow. The idea that there were photos of her from the night she'd been raped being sent around sickened me. No wonder her island kept sinking.

"She'd have to be trashed to sleep with Dan," joked Dave.

"That's not what happened—" I started to say, but Dan rebelled. My face flushed and my breath caught. I focused on pushing him back.

"Whatever," said Dave. "Everyone knows you two did it."

"I'd do her," boasted Trent.

"Cat-Lip?" asked Dave. "You serious?"

"She's got a nice body."

"Dude, she's not all that."

"I'm telling you, you've got to see these pictures."

Dan raged, and my hold began to weaken.

Luckily, Finn intervened. "Grow up, will you?" he said, glaring at the other guys. "You're acting like a bunch of sixth graders."

"We were just joking around," said Dave. "What's the big deal?"

"How would you like it if I made fun of your girl-friend?" asked Finn.

"I don't have a girlfriend."

"Exactly." Finn smiled, and several guys at the table nodded or chuckled. Immediately, the tension began to dissipate. Even Dave seemed to concede that Finn had a point.

"Don't call her Cat-Lip," Finn said. "She's Dan's girl. So we need to be nice to her. Right, Dan?"

Everyone's attention shifted to me.

I stood, not sure how much longer I could hold him off. I needed to get away. Go someplace quiet until things calmed down.

For a second, my vision blurred. I stumbled and nearly fell. Then Finn was next to me. He put his hand on my shoulder and steered me toward the edge of the cafeteria.

"Don't listen to them," he said. "They're just jealous because you got some action."

I looked at Finn, perplexed. Did he really not know what Dan had done?

"Relax, man. We're on the same team," continued Finn. "That's more important to me than some girl. Let's just forget the whole thing, okay?"

"No," I said. Cat deserved better than this. My face twitched and head jerked as I struggled with Dan.

"Look," said Finn, pitching his voice so only I could hear. "We don't need to make a bigger deal out of this than it is. What's done is done." He squeezed my shoulder. Hard. "Now, come on." He tugged me back toward the table.

"Let go," I said. Maybe I should have been grateful to Finn for helping me out, but Dan wouldn't calm down. He kept raging against me, making my head scream.

Finn's grip tightened. "I'm trying to look out for you, Danny. I throw the ball, and you catch it. That's all you got to do. That's how we win."

I was trembling now. "Let go of my arm."

"What's your problem? If anyone should be pissed, it's me," Finn said. "I'm the one she liked."

My control slipped for an instant. That's all it took. Dan's presence flooded into the gap and forced me aside. He wrenched his arm free and shoved Finn into a lunch table. Milk cartons spilled and trays clattered to the floor.

Finn scrambled to his feet. "Settle down," he ordered.

Dan's face burned. I'd never felt anything like it. His eyes narrowed and his ears throbbed with the pulse of his own blood as he charged after Finn. He'd become completely unhinged. It was like the fight in Cat's secret house, when he'd been so clumsy with rage he kicked over the candles and started the place on fire. Both moments seemed stitched together, tight as the halves of a baseball.

The whole cafeteria rumbled with shouts, but I couldn't make out what people said. All of Dan's senses were fixed on Finn.

Finn broke out of Dan's grasp and fell back, slipping on a tray. Dan jumped on him, lashing out with his fists. Pain erupted from his hand. I stayed close, trying to regain control before it was too late.

Dan kept punching Finn's head and face and chest. Finn did his best to block the blows, but several connected. The gathering crowd grew silent, stunned by Dan's violence. Finally, a security guard barged in and grabbed his arm. Then Mr. Huber helped pry Dan off of Finn. Still, the zombie struggled, spitting and twitching.

No one grabbed Finn. He got to his feet, brushed the food from his clothes, and touched his bleeding lip. He stared at the blood on his fingertips in stunned disbelief.

On the way to the principal's office, I did everything I could to take back control. Dan seemed exhausted after his outburst. He retreated some, enabling me to find a small gap. I didn't challenge him for control right away since I knew he'd overpower me. Instead, I fed his doubts, hoping to convince him to give up.

What's wrong with you? I whispered. *You're not who you think you are.*

The security guard sat Dan down in the outer office. Mr. Huber had taken Finn to a different room. Dan's breathing gradually slowed. His pulse still raced and his skin tingled, but at least he wasn't panting and twitching anymore.

Everything you do makes things worse, I whispered to Dan. *Things would be better if you weren't around.*

I think Dan knew he'd done something bad. His thoughts curled inward, and bit by bit he gave in, surrendering his body to me.

By the time Mr. Huber stepped out of Principal Murphy's office, Dan had withdrawn so much I could barely sense him.

"Principal Murphy will see you now," said the school secretary.

I nodded and stood. I would have liked more time to solidify my control, but Dan didn't put up any resistance.

Finn was already seated in the principal's office. He held an ice pack, dotted with blood, in his lap. His top lip looked swollen, and a few flecks of blood rimmed his nostrils. Other than that, he seemed okay. In fact, both he and Principal Murphy appeared unexpectedly jovial, as if they'd been swapping football stories. Finn even turned in his seat and winked at me when I entered.

"Take off your cap, Mr. Franklin," said Principal Murphy.

I removed the cap with one hand while brushing down my hair with the other.

Principal Murphy frowned. My clumsy attempt to hide the scab had only drawn more attention to it. "What happened to your head?" he asked.

"That was from before," said Finn.

"I'm asking Mr. Franklin," said Principal Murphy.

"I ran into a wall," I answered.

Principal Murphy looked unconvinced.

"I tripped," I added, although how a person might trip into a wall was beyond me.

The principal sighed and gazed at the files in front of him. "You two have been going to school together for, what, twelve years?" he asked. "And now you're both starting varsity?"

"Yes, sir," said Finn.

"This should be the time of your lives," he continued. "Your best years." He folded his hands on his desk and eyed both of us. "Now, I know you're friends, but you need to understand something very important. This school has a zero-tolerance policy for violence. Any incident results in automatic suspension as well as expulsion from all athletic teams. And Coach said we have a shot at districts this year. Maybe sectionals. So it would be a shame to lose two class leaders to a silly misunderstanding. . . ."

I realized he was giving us a way out. He wanted to let it go — brush the whole thing under the rug.

"We weren't fighting," said Finn, glancing at me. "Dan was just joking around. Right, Dan? He was showing me a wrestling move and I slipped. We're friends. We've been friends since kindergarten."

"Mr. Franklin?" said Principal Murphy, peering over the edge of his glasses at me. "Do you have anything to add?"

Dan stirred again. I couldn't tell what he thought, but one thing felt certain — if I screwed up, he would take control. And this time I might not be able to get it back.

I swallowed and tightened my grip.

"I'm not his friend," I answered, stating each word clearly.

Because I'd started the fight, I was given a suspension. Two days. I almost mouthed the verdict before Principal Murphy said it. Part of me had hoped something worse might happen — that I would get expelled or sent to juvie, and then things would really change. But no such luck. The future unfolded, relentless as fate.

Finn got off with detention because he'd only been defending himself. Principal Murphy even commended him for doing the noble thing and not tattling on me. Then Finn asked Principal Murphy to take it easy on me, saying the scuffle wasn't anything serious. No harm, no foul.

"I appreciate what you're trying to do," said Principal Murphy. "It shows a lot of character, but rules are rules. Now, get to class."

Finn thanked him and left.

I watched Finn through the window on the side of Principal Murphy's office. He paused once he reached the hall and shook his head, as if scolding me for refusing his friendship.

On my way out, I took off Dan's varsity jacket and hung it in his locker. I was pretty sure Dan would never wear it again. And neither would I.

Dan's mom was furious when she got home. The school secretary had called her at work to inform her of the suspension.

"I don't know what to do with you, Daniel," she said, pacing the kitchen. "This acting out has got to stop. Maybe I should be stricter. Is that what you want? More boundaries?"

"No," I said. "I don't think more boundaries will help."

"Then what do you want me to do?" She picked up

a dish and set it in the sink. That's the thing about Dan's mom — she always had to be *doing* something.

"I just made a mistake," I said. "It's no big deal."

"You're suspended. That goes on your transcript. What's your dad going to think?"

That Dan's a quitter, I thought, recalling the conversation Dan had with his father.

"He'll blame me," she continued.

"Why? You didn't do anything wrong."

"Is it attention? Is that what you want?"

"I don't *want* anything."

"I give up, Dan. I don't know who you are anymore. You're not acting like yourself."

That got my attention. "How should I act?" I said. "You want me to smile and work all the time and pretend everything's great like you do?"

"No. Things haven't been great in a long time."

Her response surprised me.

Dan's mom sighed and put down the sponge. "I'm sorry. I shouldn't have said that."

"It's okay."

"It's not okay. I know this past year hasn't been easy for you. Or your sister. But I want you to know that I'm trying. I really am. There's just so much I have to do —"

"You don't have to do anything for me."

"That's not true."

"I'm fine, Mom." It was the first time I'd ever called her that. "I can take care of myself."

Her expression softened. "You shouldn't have to," she said. "I'm your mom. It's my job to take care of you."

I stepped back, hating how she blamed herself for Dan's actions. "There's nothing you can do," I repeated. "Please, just let me go."

"Dan—"

I ducked into his room and locked the door.

Night

Things would have been better if I could have gotten the zombie to fall asleep, only I was too keyed up from the conversation with Dan's mom and the fight at school. I surfed the Internet and paced his room for a while. I even tried doing push-ups, but it didn't help. Sleep stayed a million miles away. Eventually I climbed out his window, unable to stand being cooped up inside a moment longer.

Going to Cat's place wasn't an option since I was still in Dan's body, so I headed downtown instead. That's when I heard the sirens. A police car approached, lights flashing and engine roaring. It rushed past and careened around a corner. I followed the sirens to see what was going on.

A fire truck, ambulance, and two police cars lined a road bisecting Main Street. Orange cones blocked off one lane, and flares burned around the accident site, casting a sickly mauve glow. Drivers slowed to see the wreck, causing traffic to back up. About a dozen people stood on the sidewalk or peered out from nearby windows and porches.

I crossed the street to get a better look. The car appeared to have missed a turn and skidded into a concrete drainage ditch. It looked like it had rolled once or twice because the windows were all broken and the roof was crushed. Skid marks snaked across both lanes. A couple firefighters circled the car, but most of the activity surrounded the ambulance where a body lay strapped to a stretcher. Two paramedics bustled around, attaching wires and tubes.

One of the paramedics, a tall guy with a shaved head, looked familiar. He'd come to Dan's house my first day here—the one who bumped his knee on the bathtub faucet while lifting the zombie.

The other paramedic, a stocky woman, worked an air bag while the tall paramedic got out a defibrillator and rubbed gel onto the electric paddles. He ripped open the guy's shirt and pressed the metal plates to pale flesh. The body twitched, then lay motionless. The tall paramedic fiddled with a few dials and gave the guy another jolt with the paddles. Both paramedics stood still, staring at a computer screen. The whole scene appeared to freeze.

Some blip or beep or other sign set them into motion again. Maybe the guy's heart had started up. The tall paramedic gave the guy a shot while the woman went back to pumping the air bag. They raised the stretcher and slid it into the brightly lit interior of the ambulance. A firefighter climbed into the back with the female paramedic. I wanted to see their brisk, urgent movements as hopeful, but they might have just been putting on a show like they would when Dan died, and as soon as the ambulance pulled away, they'd tug a sheet over the guy's face and talk about sports.

The tall paramedic shut the ambulance doors and jogged to the cab. He turned, briefly meeting my gaze before getting in. I swear he hesitated for a moment, as if he knew me.

Time sped up again and he hopped into the driver's seat. Lights flashed as the ambulance rushed away. After a block, the driver turned on the sirens, just like he'd do for Dan twelve days from now.

A tow truck arrived and pulled the car out of the ditch. Later, a policeman swept up the broken glass. Almost everyone else had left by then. The policeman seemed to resent being the last one there. He didn't do a very thorough job of sweeping. After a few minutes, he glanced

211

around and scowled at me. Then he tossed the broom and dustpan into the trunk of his squad car and drove off, leaving shards of green-edged glass sparkling in the road.

Dan wouldn't fall asleep until late that night. When I finally slipped free of him, I went straight to the Coffee Spot to meet TR. Except for a few drunk guys eating waffles, the place looked empty. TR sat in the back corner booth where Cat and her friends usually sat. He was hunched over someone's dirty cup, as if he might pick it up at any moment and take a sip.

I slid into the seat across from him. "Been here long?"

He kept staring at the coffee. I expected him to be pissed that I hadn't come earlier, but his thoughts seemed elsewhere.

"I saw you at that accident tonight," he said after a minute. "At least I saw the zombie there. It was a bad one. The guy almost died."

"How do you know he didn't?"

TR peered into the coffee mug for several seconds. I considered whether it was Cat's cup, but red lipstick stained the rim. Cat didn't wear lipstick.

"I saw a rider like us," TR said.

I straightened, wondering why he hadn't mentioned this right away. "Did you talk to him?"

TR shook his head. "He seemed dazed. Just kept staring at the body on the stretcher. I think that's where he came from."

"Came from?"

TR took a deep breath. "I think we're them," he said. "The corpses. I think we come from them — like we're bits of their soul or something, and we broke off. And now we're echoing back."

"That's ridiculous."

"Don't tell me you've never thought about it," said TR.

I had, of course, but that didn't mean it was true. *"I'm. Not. Dan."* I stood and walked through the wall into the parking lot.

TR followed me out. "That's exactly how I felt at first. Like I'd ever want to be Waster. But then I thought, what if the reason Waster acts the way he does is *because* I broke off," he said. "What if he gets drunk all the time and crashed his truck *because* he lost me?"

"Look, even if I was once part of Dan, I'm not anymore. I'm my own person now." I cut through the back lot and headed toward Cat's place.

"You're not the only one who's done bad things," said TR.

I slowed, not sure what he was talking about. I hadn't done anything bad. Granted, losing control and letting

Dan attack Finn hadn't been good. And harassing Cat with the figurines was a mistake. But I'd fix that. Ever since I'd arrived, all I'd tried to do was make things better.

"Waster messed up, too," continued TR. "He did something terrible. It's not easy for me to admit that I'm him—that *I* messed up like that. But maybe it's the only answer."

I kept walking.

TR jogged to catch up with me. "The rider I saw merged back into the guy," he said.

"So? That doesn't prove anything. We get pulled back into the corpses every morning."

"Yeah, but this was different. This rider didn't fight it. Instead, it was like he surrendered himself. And then everything was okay," said TR. "The guy's heart started to beat again."

"Don't be stupid," I said. "If you surrender like that, you're done. Waster will take over, and you'll be lost. No more TR."

TR nodded, seeming to agree with me. We passed through some bushes into a neighborhood.

"What if that's the sacrifice we need to make?" he asked.

I couldn't believe this. After all we'd been through, was he trying to convince me to give up? "Waster isn't going to make things right," I told him. "And neither will the zombie. *They're* the ones who messed things up. That's why we have to take over completely, so we can undo what they did."

TR paused. I turned to see why he'd stopped.

"Do you ever wonder if maybe, instead of saving Cat, you're supposed to save Dan?" he asked.

"Dan's dead. Or he will be. He doesn't deserve to be saved. I'm glad he's going to kill himself."

"Why?"

"Because the world's better off without him."

"You really hate him that much?" asked TR.

I thought of all the suffering Dan had caused—not just the rape, but the empty, self-absorbed way he went through life. The first thing I'd seen, coming into this life, was Dan turning his back on it and hurting everyone who cared about him. "Hate is a mild way of putting it."

TR shook his head. "You have to forgive yourself, Dan."

I clenched my fists, wanting to punch TR. But what was the point? My hand would just pass through him. "Don't ever call me that again," I said. "You might think it's okay to give up, but I don't."

I cut through a yard to get to Cat's apartment faster.

TR didn't follow me.

Part III

Sunday, November 2

"What's wrong with your head?" asked Teagan. She stood in the doorway, mouth agape. For some reason, she looked younger.

"It's makeup," I replied. "From Halloween." I don't know why I said it. She'd know soon enough it wasn't true. Lying for no reason was something Dan would do.

"Did you get in a fight?" she asked.

"Shhh . . ." I glanced at the doorway, afraid their mom would hear.

"Mom's gone, genius," said Teagan. "Day two of her sales conference, remember?"

"Right." I checked the clock on the bedside table: 10:43 a.m. I'd wasted most of the morning sleeping. Only two days left to figure things out before the past was set.

"Is that why you wore that stupid hat yesterday?" asked Teagan, pointing to my forehead.

"Don't you have something better to do?"

"Nope. It's Sunday. The only thing on my list today is to bother you." She perched on Dan's desk and grinned. "Did someone kick your ass at Finn's party?"

Dan stirred. "What do you know about Finn's party?"

"I know it was pretty wild," said Teagan. "And I know you were there."

"Did you go?"

She squinted at me like I'd just asked if turtles could fly. "Who'd invite me? You?"

"No. I'm glad that you didn't go."

"Thanks, dear brother. I like spending time with you, too."

"That's not what I meant," I said. "The party wasn't much fun is all. It was a waste of time."

Teagan scoffed. "You don't have to worry about me embarrassing you. It's not like any of your friends would talk to me."

"They'd talk to you," I said, remembering how Finn had said hello to her outside of school. Then again, for

Teagan that was a week from now. "Why would you want to hang out with them, anyway?"

"Doesn't everyone want to hang out with them?" mocked Teagan. "And dress like them? And *be* them? I should try out for cheerleading, then Kendra and I could be BFFs." She flipped her hair back, imitating Kendra. "I think I'll dye my hair blue. Or black. That would look cool, wouldn't it?"

"Yeah. That will make you real popular," I joked.

Teagan's shoulders slumped. I realized she'd been asking seriously. That's why she looked younger—her hair hadn't been dyed yet, and she wasn't wearing dark makeup around her eyes.

"You should dye it," I told her. "Black would look good on you."

"Whatever."

"I mean it."

She straightened slightly. "Does that mean you'll drive me to the drugstore? You owe me."

"I do?"

"For not taking me to my eye appointment yesterday. If I go blind, it's your fault."

"You're not going blind," I said. "Trust me."

"Can I drive, then?"

"No."

"How about this? Take me to the drugstore and then we can get donuts like we used to," said Teagan. "Remember those Sunday mornings when Dad would get a dozen different donuts, and he'd cut them up so we could taste each one? I loved that."

"I'm not even dressed."

"So get dressed. Mom left us money."

I wanted to say yes. It would have been fun to spend the day with her, but that would only make things harder for her. Until I changed things, I had to keep Dan away from the people I cared about. "I'm not getting donuts," I said.

"Why not? You found your car, didn't you?"

I frowned, not sure what she was referring to.

"You could get one of those Bavarian cream thingies," she continued. "That's your favorite, right? We need donuts!"

"Just eat cereal for breakfast."

"Cereal sucks," said Teagan. "Please. I can't go to the store without you."

"Ride your bike there."

"My bike's broken."

"Then walk," I said, annoyed. "I'm not your chauffeur."

Her face barely moved, but the change in her was like

metal shutters slamming over storefront windows. "Forget it," she muttered. "I'll get someone else to take me."

Teagan left shortly after that. She must have walked to the store, because she was gone for over two hours. When she came home, she blasted her music and dyed her hair. I avoided her for the rest of the day, but I didn't have to see her to know that she'd chosen black instead of blue.

Night

Once Dan was safely asleep, I slipped out to find TR. I felt bad about our argument the night before, and I needed to talk with someone after staying isolated all day.

TR wasn't waiting for me outside of Dan's house, so I went to the Coffee Spot. When he didn't show up there, I tried Cat's house. She was curled up in bed already, while her dad sat alone on the couch, watching a movie—their Sunday-night ritual derailed. A bowl of popcorn sat in the hall outside her door.

I stayed with her for a while, but I kept wondering where TR might be. The thought that something bad might have happened to him kept nagging at me. I finally left Cat's apartment and wandered up and down Main Street, looking for TR. Then I checked the buildings we used to jump off of. I even went to the radio tower we'd climbed, but no dice.

Come on, TR. Where are you?

Bits of the conversation we'd had the other night haunted my thoughts—TR's talk of letting go and merging back into Waster. So what if he'd tried to do that, and now he couldn't get out? He might be trapped in Waster. Or worse. Every time I'd let myself sink into Dan's thoughts, I'd had this sense that if I went too far, I wouldn't be able to call myself back. I'd be swept away until I drowned in his whispers. All we had was our sense of ourselves as something separate, and if we lost that, then what?

I wandered around town for hours, but I didn't find TR anywhere. If I could have, I would have gone to Waster's house, except I'd never walked TR home. I hadn't even asked where Waster lived. Why hadn't I tried to find out more about him when I had the chance? It made me wonder how many other things there were that I might not learn until it was too late.

Then the reeling hit.

Saturday, November 1

It came fast, pulling me in a different direction than I was used to. Houses blurred by, melting into a sickening gray tunnel that ended at Dan.

I opened my eyes, unable to make sense of what I saw. Dark sky with darker shadows loomed overhead. The smell of burning oil hung in the air. I clawed the ground, afraid to move. A horn blared. The shadows blurring past ten or twenty feet above coalesced into train cars.

Dan bristled. I held him off, but it wasn't easy. A nauseating sea of pain engulfed me. In order to stay in control, I had to feel every bit of it. *This is me,* I whispered to myself. *This pain is mine.*

Long after the train passed, my ears rang and my head continued to ache. The patches of sky I glimpsed through the tracks glistened with stars. I tried to get up, but a surge of dizziness sent me sprawling onto my hands and knees. My fingers splashed between wet rocks at the edge of a river, and my sleeves grew heavy with water. I sat back, trying to collect myself.

Dirt clung to something sticky on my cheek. Tar maybe? I wiped off what I could. The thick liquid shimmered on my fingertips. I tasted a drop and my mouth filled with the coppery tang of blood. Then I touched my forehead and all the pain I felt funneled to one spot, making me wince.

Dan immediately shot in to take control.

Get a grip, I told myself. *Cat needs you. This is why you're here.*

I sank deeper into the pain. My jaw clenched, and my breath came in short, shuddering gasps. Connecting to Dan's body was like pressing my head to a hot burner, but it was the only way to close the gap. *You are not who you think you are,* I whispered to Dan. *You're a rapist. A monster. To fix this, you must die.*

At last, Dan weakened. I focused on keeping him distant while I solidified my control.

Gradually, the pain eased and my vision steadied, allowing me to take stock of my surroundings. I was sitting beneath a train trestle that spanned a shallow river. It was an area I recognized from one of my nighttime adventures with TR.

I stood, taking care not to bump my head on the lower beams of the train trestle or stumble on the slick ground. The river seemed mostly dry. Only a small trickle of water worked its way through the stony bed. I climbed a dirt path on the overgrown bank to the road. The sky slanted to dark blue near the horizon, where light from the rising sun drowned out some of the stars.

With a cautious hand, I felt my head again to see how bad the wound was. The blood had become sticky in places while in others it had dried, making me itch. At most, the wound seemed an hour or two old. I still had no idea what had caused it or what had brought me to these tracks.

I followed the road back to town. At one point, I passed a man walking a dog and turned to hide the blood on my face, but the man didn't appear concerned. He said, "Good morning," and nodded. I had on a skeleton shirt, so he might have thought the blood was part of my costume. To him, this was the morning after Halloween.

The sky continued to lighten, revealing traces of the night's activities—pumpkins smashed in the street and ribbons of toilet paper hanging from tree branches. I spotted Dan's car parked in front of a house I didn't recognize. It was a big place, with a three-car garage and finely manicured bushes, situated in what Dan's mom would call a "nice neighborhood," even though beer cans littered the front yard and broken bottles glistened on the sidewalk.

I found keys in Dan's pocket and unlocked the door, not sure how his car had gotten here. There were so many things I still needed to figure out.

When I got to Dan's house, I didn't pull into the driveway. All the lights were off, so I didn't think anyone would notice if I drove around a little longer. I went to Cat's neighborhood and considered going up to her window, but if she spotted me looking in, all bloody-faced and creepy, it wouldn't be good. Eventually I drove on. If only I could start over someplace else—go to Dan's dad's house and live with his perfect kids and adoring wife. Except the next morning I'd just get pulled back here again.

I did a U-turn and drove to the side of town where I thought TR lived. Then I wound back and forth on the narrow, cracked streets, looking for something that might lead me to him. The fact that he hadn't shown up last night worried me. For the first time since I'd arrived, I felt completely alone. TR was the only one I could talk to about what was going on. The only one who understood. I had to find him.

Other than the occasional porch light, the houses on both sides of the street remained dark. Several had windows that were boarded up, and most needed new paint. All the houses looked about the same size and shape, pushed together like shoe boxes on a shelf — what Dan's mom would call the "wrong side of the tracks."

I kept driving through the cracked streets, searching for TR, until the engine sputtered and Dan's car coasted to a stop. I pumped the gas and turned the key a few times, but nothing happened. The fuel gauge pointed to *E*. Crap. There'd been half a tank the other day. Then again, that was tomorrow.

The sun stretched above the horizon now, and the sky looked clear and blue. I made sure to tug the hood over my forehead before leaving Dan's car to walk home. As bad as I felt, dizzy with pain and hunger and a lack of sleep, I had to admit it was a pretty morning.

By the time I crossed Main Street, a lot of people were out walking their dogs or getting coffee. Every time I saw someone, I felt like they were staring at me. Maybe they saw the blood and knew it wasn't fake. Or maybe they could tell that I was an impostor, living a life that wasn't mine.

I spied Dan's mom through the kitchen window before going into the house. She must have gotten up early for the conference Teagan had mentioned. Hopefully, she'd leave soon.

I snuck around to the side and tried Dan's window. Sure enough, it had been left unlatched and the screen was easy to remove. I climbed in, ruffled the bed to make it look like I'd slept there in case his mom checked it, then ducked into the bathroom and turned on the shower.

The warm water made my head sting. Still, it felt good to wash the blood off my face. Water swirled pink around my toes, reminding me of the blood I'd seen my first day here. It didn't look as pretty now. No fields of red tulips blooming or rose petals curling—just dirty water and a lot of pain.

Someone knocked on the door. I turned off the shower and grabbed a towel. "Hold on," I said. "I'm getting dressed."

"I'm late," replied Dan's mom. "I should have left five minutes ago."

"Okay." I think she was waiting for me to come out, but I knew better than to open the door.

After a few seconds, she continued. "I left some money on the counter for food. And remember to take your sister to her eye appointment today."

"I will," I told her, although it felt like a lie.

Dan's mom lingered in the hall. Was she waiting for

me to say something else? I stood, silent and dripping, on the other side of the door.

"I'll keep my cell on in case you need anything." Her footsteps receded. A few minutes later, the garage door rumbled open and shut.

I dried off, careful not to stain the towel with blood. Maybe I should have asked when the appointment was, but given Teagan's complaint about missing her eye appointment, I doubted I'd take her. Their mom would reschedule for two weeks from now. In fact, that's where they'd be when Dan slashed his wrists.

The eye appointment! I thought. If I got Teagan to it today, then she and her mom wouldn't go out two weeks from now. They'd stay home, so Dan couldn't kill himself then. Of course, he'd probably still find a way to off himself, but at least Teagan wouldn't return home with itchy eyes and barge into the bathroom to discover her brother bleeding in the tub. I could spare her that. All I had to do was get her to the appointment.

Except I didn't have Dan's car.

I pulled on some pants and hurried out. Taking Teagan to her appointment wouldn't fix everything, but at least it was a start—something simple and easy to change. It might even be the lever I was looking for. Changing this could set off a chain reaction that might help me change other things.

I found a large, empty gas can in the garage. Darting back inside, I grabbed Dan's wallet and pulled on a tattered cap to hide the wound on his forehead. "Be back in a little while," I shouted to Teagan.

People looked at me funny as I jogged to the gas station carrying the red gas can, but no one said anything. I filled the can and paid inside, not waiting for change. Then I raced back to where I'd left Dan's car. At least I ran to where I'd thought I'd left Dan's car, only I couldn't find it. The narrow, cracked streets and small houses all looked the same to me. Guess I should have checked a street sign that morning. The one landmark I remembered was a church with two square steeples a little farther down the block from where I'd parked.

A couple guys sitting on porch steps eyed me as I approached. I decided to ask them about the church. The guys looked older, but not by much. A third guy was hunched over the hood of a truck in the driveway.

"You got a problem, man?" asked one of the guys. Despite the chill air, he had on a tank top that showed off the tattoos darkening his arms.

"Yeah," I said. "I lost my car."

He smirked. "So? You think we have it?"

"No. I thought you might be able to help me."

The guy chuckled and looked at his friend, as if to say, *Can you believe this freak?* Seeing a skinny white kid running around the neighborhood with a bright-red gas can probably wasn't normal.

"You check the lost and found?" asked his friend.

Both guys snickered. Talking to them started to seem like a dumb idea.

"What's the big fuss?" asked the tank-top guy. "It's just a car. You probably lose them all the time."

"I really need to find it," I said.

"I think you're lost, *cabrón*," he replied. "You shouldn't be here."

"That's right. You need to go to the help desk," joked his friend.

The guy working on the truck straightened up. I couldn't see his face, but I immediately recognized his stocky, triangular frame.

Waster!

I could have hugged him, except the other guys were there, so I settled for an enthusiastic nod instead.

Waster nodded back. "It's okay," he called to the guys on the steps. "I know this guy." He wiped his hand on a rag and came over to talk with me. "You go to Jefferson, right?"

"Yeah," I said, unable to stop grinning.

"Me, too," he said. "I think I've seen you there before."

No kidding, I almost replied, but I figured TR wanted to play it cool in front of the guys on the steps.

234

"What you up to?" I asked, throwing in a wink for good measure.

"Fixing my truck." He tucked the rag into his back pocket. "I'm Terc," he said, thrusting out his hand.

I shook his hand and winked again, but he didn't wink back or pick his nose or do anything strange. "Terc? That's an odd name," I said. "Anyone ever call you TR?"

"No. Just Terc," he said. "It's short for Tercio. It means warrior. Actually, it's a whole legion of warriors. My dad was ambitious, you know?"

I thought he might be speaking in code, trying to tell me something. "So what are you a warrior for?"

"Fuck if I know." Half his mouth curled up in a goofy, lopsided grin. It was exactly the sort of expression TR would make before he jumped off a bridge or stepped in front of a semi.

I scratched my nose and tugged my ear, hoping TR would give me some signal back. But Terc just stood there, watching my odd behavior. "You okay, dude?" he asked.

The sound of a car approaching, its windows rattling with loud music, interrupted our talk. Terc looked past me as the car stopped in front of the house. Its chrome rims shined in the late-morning sun. The two guys from the steps sauntered over to talk with the driver. Once the music was turned down, Terc glanced back at me.

"TR?" I said.

He frowned. "Dude, I told you—it's just Terc."

A little kid, maybe three or four years old, teetered down the steps and ran over to us. He must have been playing on the porch behind the two guys. In his hand, he clutched a bright-green plastic action figure. He darted around Terc, grabbing his pant leg.

Terc looked embarrassed. "This is Mateo," he said, shifting to keep his pants from falling down. "My cousin's kid. She's out right now."

Mateo peered at me from behind Terc. I thought of the funeral TR had mentioned—the one Waster's mom had made him attend. The one with the small, fancy coffin. Kid-sized.

"You going to burn something down?" Terc asked.

The question startled me until I realized he was referring to the gas can.

"My car ran out of gas," I said, shaking the can. "It's somewhere around here, but I can't remember where."

"Dude, I thought I had a bad memory." He flashed his goofy, lopsided grin again. Other than that, there was no trace of TR. Terc didn't even act like Waster anymore. He wasn't stoned or drunk, and he seemed more awake than I'd ever seen him. If not for the grin, I would have thought I had the wrong guy.

"You should be careful walking around here," Terc said.

The car honked. "Terc! You coming?" called the driver. Both guys from the porch had gotten in.

Terc started to move, but Mateo still clung to his leg, nearly tripping him. "I can't," he shouted back. "I got to watch the kid until my cousin comes home."

"Put him inside," called the tank-top guy. "We won't be gone long."

Terc looked at the house, then back at the car.

"You can turn on the TV," the guy urged. "He'll be fine."

"Sorry, man," Terc answered. "I'm supposed to stay here."

Supposed to stay here. Terc's words sounded ordinary enough, but they stuck with me.

TR had always teased me for claiming to know what I was *supposed to do.* Yet all along, maybe he'd wanted to know what he was supposed to do. So was this his purpose — to stay with the kid and keep him from wandering into the street and getting hit by a car? Had TR found the thing he needed to fix?

The guys teased Terc, but he wouldn't back down. After a few minutes, they cursed and drove off.

I studied Terc, sensing once again that Waster was different. My attention must have made him nervous, though, because he went back to the truck. Mateo darted around his legs, begging to hold a screwdriver. "Good luck finding your car, man," he said.

"Thanks," I replied. "Take care, TR."

He laughed and shook his head. "It's just Terc."

I found Dan's car two streets over and poured in the gas. The engine sputtered, coming to life on the fourth try. After filling up at a gas station, I raced home.

"Teagan!" I called the moment I entered. "When's your eye appointment?"

"Half an hour ago," she replied, squinting at the TV. A bowl of cereal rested in her lap.

"Did you go?"

She clanked her spoon against the bowl and frowned. "How could I? You were supposed to drive me."

"I had to find my car."

"Nice hat," said Teagan.

I tugged Dan's hat down over his forehead. The brim of it grated the wound, jabbing me with pain.

"Mom's going to be pissed."

"I know," I said. "Believe me, I know."

Night

I checked on Teagan first. She was huddled on the floor of her bedroom, messing around on Facebook. It wasn't only her light-brown hair that made her look younger. It was that her features held no trace of the storm to come, the way the sky could be clear and calm hours before a tornado touched down. In a few days, she'd defend her brother, then hate him, then find him bleeding to death in the tub—a cruel sequence of events that would tear her apart.

On the other side of her bedroom wall, Dan's mom lay in bed with a cookbook, dog-earing recipes. Whatever would happen the next day wasn't just about Cat. The fates of countless others hung in the balance—Teagan's, their mom's, Tricia's, Trent's, Finn's—one action echoing through hundreds of lives. If I failed to set things right, I'd let them all down.

I went to Terc's place after that. There was still no sign of TR. Mateo lay curled up in a sleeping bag on the floor in front of the TV, clutching his green action figure, while "just Terc" slept on the couch. One of Terc's arms dangled over the edge so his thick hand rested protectively on Mateo's shoulder.

Terc might not have looked anything like TR, yet something about the expression on his sleeping face made me think of my friend. So was he in there still? Or had he sacrificed himself to make things right? Mateo was alive and well. He hadn't wandered into the road and gotten killed by a car. I wished I could congratulate TR on changing things. Mostly, though, I just missed my friend.

I searched for Cat last. She wasn't at the Coffee Spot or her secret house or her room.

I found her sitting on the floor of her dad's closet, sketching the self-portrait I'd seen her take down the first day I'd met her. Only now the portrait wasn't complete. The version of herself as Alice sat at the head of the table, bold and confident, but that was all she'd drawn. As I watched, she added the March Hare to the foreground—a frightened, animalistic counterpoint to Alice's poise. Then she drew herself as the little Dormouse in the teapot, appearing half drowned and smaller than I remembered. Finally, she sketched the Mad Hatter. This was the figure she seemed to struggle the most with drawing.

Her eyes welled up and her hand trembled as she outlined the Mad Hatter's top hat, making it so big it nearly swallowed her head and cast a shadow across half her face. The smile she gave herself looked overly cheerful, to the point of being deranged. And the eyes she drew seemed more angry than happy. The Hatter stared intently at a teacup, which she depicted as overflowing, even while the Hatter's hand tilted to pour more cream in.

Above the whole scene, she sketched the horizontal crescent moon of the Cheshire Cat's grin. Before, I'd seen the grin in an optimistic light, but now it appeared menacing—a pendulum about to slice the table in half.

So which one was Cat? Would she be the scared March Hare? The sad little Dormouse? The deranged Mad Hatter? Or the bold girl who falls into a hole?

I stayed with Cat until she put away the portrait and went to sleep. I still didn't know exactly what would happen or what I should do to fix things. I just knew that tomorrow—Dan's yesterday—was my last chance to set things right. The day of the party.

The day I had to change.

Friday, October 31

The wall was blank. I pulled the calendar off its nail, thinking I must have missed something. Where the messages had been, not a scratch remained.

I checked the other walls, pulling back Dan's posters and looking behind his closet door, desperate to find something that would tell me what to do. Beneath the clutter, all I found were sterile, mute barriers. I was on my own.

The message wasn't the only thing that had vanished. When I went to the bathroom, I discovered that the wound on the zombie's forehead had disappeared as well.

Not so much as a scar or bruise marked where it had been. I spent a good ten minutes in the shower, reveling in the warm patter of water against my face.

After shaving and dressing, I returned to the problem of the blank wall in a much better mood. The calendar sat on Dan's bed. It had been flipped to October, not November, so the picture at the top differed from the one I'd gotten used to seeing. The new photo depicted a salmon swimming up a waterfall, launching itself into the waiting jaws of a grizzly bear. PERSEVERANCE, read the caption. *Some succeed by sticking with it. Others meet their end this way.*

I switched the calendar back to November, preferring the comparatively upbeat photo of the gazelle jumping over the crocodile.

"You still thinking about Thanksgiving?" asked Teagan from the doorway. She nodded to the calendar.

I shrugged.

"If it worries you so much, don't go," she said.

I noticed the dates outlined in pen with *visit Dad* written across them. It was the only thing marked in November, but Dan wouldn't make it that far.

"Don't go," she repeated. "Spend the week with us. It's not like Dad will care."

"That's it!" I said. "Teagan, you're a genius!"

She scowled, probably thinking I was being sarcastic.

"I'm only trying to help," she said. "You don't have to be a jerk about it."

As soon as she left, I rifled through the drawer of Dan's desk for his pocket knife. Then I carved two words deep into the wall so they couldn't be erased.

DON'T GO!

I stepped back to admire my work. It's hard to explain how much those words comforted me. When the wall had been blank, I'd been lost—a ship without a rudder. But with something there, I had purpose. Direction. The fact that I'd carved the words into the wall myself seemed negligible. After all, who's to say something larger wasn't working through me, using my hand to send me the messages? And it wasn't like I'd thought up the words myself. Teagan had. I'd merely recognized their significance.

DON'T GO! was the perfect solution. I knew Dan had been at the party—several people had seen him there. So if I kept the zombie from going tonight, then Dan couldn't possibly hurt Cat. There was no way around that fact. And no way to misinterpret such a simple, blunt message. Even if a blow to the zombie's head scrambled my memory, or if Cat wanted to meet Dan somewhere else, the words I'd carved into the wall would stop me from going. All I had to do was follow this one simple message—DON'T GO!— and things would change. They had to.

I put the calendar back and skipped into the kitchen to eat breakfast. Midway through a surprisingly pleasing bowl of cornflakes, Dan's cell phone vibrated with a text from Finn.

Pick me up in ten.

I stared at the text, trying to decipher its meaning. It was Friday, October 31. Maybe Dan gave Finn a ride to school on Fridays. But then why send a text reminding him? Besides, the tone of the text seemed imperative, suggesting that something important was taking place.

I hurried to finish breakfast and brush my teeth. Then I grabbed Dan's backpack and headed out.

"Where are you going?" called Dan's mom.

"School," I said.

"Aren't you taking Teagan?"

Hearing her name, Teagan drifted into the kitchen. She'd just showered and her hair dripped water onto her shirt.

"I can't," I said. "I have to pick up Finn."

Their mom set her coffee mug down and put her hands on her hips. "Stick her in the backseat, then," she said. "There's room."

"I'm not luggage," protested Teagan.

"I said the back, honey. Not the trunk."

Dan's phone vibrated again. Another text from Finn.

??????

"I'm late. I have to go now," I said.

"Then how's Teagan going to get to school?"

Teagan gave her mom an annoyed look.

"She's your daughter," I said. "You'll find a way."

At first, I wasn't sure where to go to pick up Finn, until I remembered the house in the "nice neighborhood" where I'd found Dan's car parked the other day. That must be where the Halloween party would happen, so that would be Finn's place.

After sending Finn a text to let him know I was on my way, I focused on the landmarks around me, retracing my steps to his street. Over the past two weeks, leaves had floated back up to the trees, turning from brown to gold and red. Their colors appeared all the brighter after having seen their loss. Even the leaves on the ground had changed from how they'd been when I'd first arrived — going from drab wet piles to swirling drifts of orange and yellow, while the smashed jack-o'-lanterns I'd seen rotting in the road now sat plump on porches, flaunting gap-toothed grins.

If I continued backwards long enough, all the leaves would return to their branches and the trees would become lush with summer. But if I failed to change things tonight — if I let Dan hurt Cat — I wouldn't be able to take that back.

I pulled into Finn's driveway. The yard didn't have beer cans in it yet. Still, the manicured bushes and ostentatious three-car garage were unmistakable. Finn came out and slid into the passenger seat.

"About time," he said. "Go that way. We need to pick up Trent."

I drove in the direction he indicated. "So, you ready?" I asked.

"For what?"

"Tonight," I said, trying to find out everything I could about what lay ahead. "The party."

"Hold up," said Finn. "You just drove past it."

"Oh. Right." I stopped the car, not sure which side of the road Trent's house was on.

Finn chuckled. "Wake up, Dan. You need some coffee?"

"Yeah." I feigned a yawn. Better he think I was tired than clueless.

Trent came out and hopped into the backseat. "No truck?" he asked Finn, clearly not used to Dan picking him up.

"My brother borrowed it to get the kegs," said Finn. "I hope people bring some money for the cover—those things are expensive."

Trent leaned through the gap between the seats. "How much you charging?"

247

"Five bucks," said Finn. "Except for girls. They drink free."

"Even ugly girls?"

"I make no such crass distinctions," replied Finn, taking on a lofty tone. "All ladies are welcome at my party. But," he added, "try to be a little selective with who you invite. I'd rather not have a bunch of freshies puking in my yard."

"What if they're hot freshies?" asked Trent. "Like Dan's sister."

"She's not coming," I said.

"Why not? I thought she was your date."

"Very funny," I muttered, trying not to let Trent get to me. I couldn't risk provoking Dan.

"So, who are you bringing?" asked Finn.

"No one," I said.

"Because you're bringing your sister?" quipped Trent.

I shrugged.

"Seriously," asked Finn. "Who do you want to hook up with?"

"I don't want to hook up with anyone," I replied, turning into the school parking lot.

"Dan, Dan, Dan," said Finn. "As your friend, I can't allow you to wallow in self-pity at the best party of the year. We need to find you a girl."

"How about Kendra?" asked Trent. "She's stacked."

"'Stacked'?" I said.

"Or Bella," he pressed. "Or Laney. Take your pick."

"I'm not into them," I said.

"Then, who?"

Without intending to, I thought of Cat. Several seconds passed before I realized I was staring at the flagpole where she usually hung out with Tricia. I glanced down and fiddled with the car keys. "No one," I repeated.

"Really?" pressed Finn. "Then who were you just staring at?"

"I wasn't staring."

"Yes, you were. You're even trembling." He peered across the parking lot at the flagpole. "It's her, isn't it? The girl with the purple hair?"

"Cat-Lip?" asked Trent. "*That's* who you like?"

"Don't call her that," I said.

Finn and Trent looked at each other.

"You've got it bad, my friend," said Finn. "You should go ask her."

"No. No way."

"Come on, Dan. It's easy. Want me to do it?" Finn reached for the door handle.

My heart kicked. "Don't!"

He raised an eyebrow. "So, are you going to ask her out?"

"Maybe," I said. "Not right now."

Finn sighed. "When are you going to learn, Danny boy? There's no time like the present." He shoved open the door. "Hey, Cat!" he shouted. About a hundred students looked over—Finn knew how to command an audience. "Dan wants to ask you something."

I grabbed Finn's jacket and tugged him back, but it was too late. Everyone was already staring at us, including Cat.

"It's nothing," I yelled. "Forget it."

Behind me, I heard Trent giggling.

I waited until Cat walked away with Tricia, then I turned to glare at Finn.

"Relax, man," he said. "I'm helping you out. Just wait—you'll see."

I managed to steer clear of Cat for most of the day, even skipping biology class so I wouldn't see her. It went against every instinct to avoid her like this. Usually, I spent all my time looking for her, but today was too important to risk rocking the boat. After tonight I could spend all the time I wanted with Cat. I wouldn't have to worry about Dan hurting her. I'd be past it. I might even be able to take over completely. Just keep away from Cat for one more day and things would change—it was as simple as that.

When the final period ended, I zipped Dan's backpack shut and hurried for the door, nearly home free.

"Hi, Dan," said Cat. She must have been waiting in the hall for me.

"Excuse me." I tried to edge past her, but she wouldn't let me go.

"I thought there was something you wanted to ask me."

I shook my head. It hadn't occurred to me that Cat might look for me. Even after all those nights watching her, she still managed to surprise me.

"So I suppose all that ruckus in the parking lot this morning was just in my head?" she continued, the slightest hint of a smile turning up the corners of her mouth. "Another figment of my overactive imagination?"

"We were joking around," I said.

"Oh. I see." Her smile fell. She probably thought Dan and his friends had been making fun of her, calling her Cat-Lip like everyone else.

"We weren't joking about you," I added.

"Of course not." Her eyes narrowed, and she clasped her binder to her chest.

I noticed a crescent-shaped grin drawn beneath two slit eyes on the back of her hand. "Is that the Cheshire Cat?"

"Changing the subject," she observed. "Smooth."
"Really?"
"No. But you get points for being right about this."

She indicated the drawing on her hand. "Are you a Dodgson fan?"

"You mean Charles Dodgson?" I asked, recalling the name from something I'd seen in her room one night. "That's Lewis Carroll's real name, right?"

"Well done, Mr. Franklin. Most of the time no one gets what I'm talking about."

"Their loss," I said. "So why do you admire Dodgson so much?"

"What makes you so certain I do?"

"Don't you?"

"If I didn't know better, I'd think you'd been spying on me."

My pulse sped up and my skin prickled. A wave of vertigo rushed through me. What was I thinking, talking to her like this? If Dan sensed what I was doing . . . "I should get going."

"He was creative," said Cat. "Not just in writing, but in everything he did."

I paused.

"He invented hundreds of things," she continued. "A device for taking notes in the dark, and a card for measuring drinks, and tournament rules for tennis. He went through life creating things no one else thought of. But he stammered so badly that most people thought he was dumb. Nobody saw who he really was."

"I know what that's like," I said.

Cat tilted her head. Dan wasn't exactly the misunderstood-genius type, so my comment probably confused her. She studied me for several seconds. "You're different from the others," she concluded.

"What others?"

"Sorry—that came out wrong. Sometimes I talk too much. 'That's the effect of living backwards. It always makes one a little giddy at first.'"

"What did you say?"

"It's a quote from *Through the Looking-Glass*. The White Queen tells Alice that it's a poor sort of memory that only works one way." She shrugged. "I quote things when I'm nervous."

As had happened before, the first day I'd seen her, I got the sense that she could see beyond Dan's exterior to who I truly was. "I don't mean to make you nervous," I said.

She smiled, and her gaze deepened. "You probably do a lot of things you don't mean to do."

God, it felt amazing to be seen by her.

"You ask her yet, Danny?" interrupted Finn.

The slam of lockers and bustle of bodies in the hall called me back. I'd been so focused on Cat that I'd forgotten where I was. Or what I was supposed to do. Finn gave me a wry grin, seeming to know I'd lost track of things.

Cat's demeanor instantly changed. If she'd been

nervous around me, that was nothing compared to how she acted now. She fidgeted, unable to meet Finn's gaze but unable to look away, either. "Ask me what?"

"To my Halloween party. Dan was hoping you'd come. He didn't mention that?"

"No."

"I hadn't gotten around to it yet," I said, feeling sick. Things were spiraling out of control. Cat might go to the party now. I never should have talked to her.

"Well, don't let me ruin the surprise," joked Finn. "Maybe I'll see you there. Wear a costume."

Cat didn't say anything in response, but the way her cheeks flushed spoke volumes.

"I'll leave you two lovebirds to it, then," said Finn.

"We're not—" started Cat, but Finn was already several steps away. He glanced back and smirked at her quick denial, then continued down the hall, leaving the two of us to sort it out.

It suddenly became clear to me what I had to do. Keeping Dan from the party wasn't enough. There was one more step I needed to take.

"Sorry about that," I said.

"Don't be. So, you were about to ask me something?"

"Right." I swallowed, fighting down my panic.

Students eyed us as they walked past, while inside, Dan pressed against me. There were roles we had to play.

Expectations to fulfill. "Would you like to go to Finn's party?" I asked, determined to deliver my lines as credibly as possible.

"I don't know." Cat's gaze drifted past me to where Finn had gone. "It's not exactly my scene."

"Oh."

"That's it?" she said. "You're not going to try to convince me?"

"How about this: I think you should go," I said. "I think you'll have fun."

"Fun, huh? What if I don't like fun?"

"Then, I know some really boring people you can talk with. They'll be there, too."

"Tempting. Will you pick me up?"

I wanted to say yes. I would have given anything to be able to drive to her house and start over someplace else with her. But the future would never change so easily.

"I can't," I lied. "My car broke down. Why don't I meet you there? Around eight?"

"Okay. Eight it is." By now the hall had mostly cleared out. She started to leave.

"Bye, Cat," I said. "Take care of yourself."

"You'll see me in a few hours," she said.

No, I thought. *I won't.* Only I couldn't say this.

I did my best to smile as she walked away.

*   *   *

Finn and Trent were waiting for me in the parking lot when I finally came out. They talked about the party. I had trouble focusing on anything they said. I didn't even realize I was biting my cheek until the taste of blood filled my mouth.

Trent gave me directions as we left the parking lot. I cranked up the radio and turned when he told me to. We ended up at a duplex on the edge of town where they needed to pick up some "stuff" for the party.

"Wait here," Trent said after I pulled over. "This might take a few."

He got out, leaving Finn and me alone in the car. Finn leaned back and propped a foot on the dashboard, nodding to the music.

"So, you really like Cat?" he asked after a minute.

I traced his profile, from his straight brown hair to his boyish features and strong jaw. He stared ahead at the road, nervously tapping his fingers to the music. The confidence that usually surrounded him seemed eggshell-thin.

"Why do you want to know?"

Finn shrugged, as if the question didn't matter. "You can have your pick of girls, and you're interested in her. Makes me wonder why."

I took a deep breath. "She's different," I said.

"What do you mean?"

"It's like other girls are roses or daisies or daffodils.

They're pretty but ordinary," I told him. "Cat's something else entirely. She's an orchid growing in a swamp. You could spend your whole life never knowing the orchid's there. But once you see her, nothing ever looks the same."

I thought Finn might make fun of my poetic explanation, but he didn't. If he hadn't noticed Cat before, he would now. "She sounds pretty incredible."

"She is. More than you know."

"You must really be into her," he added.

"Yeah. Well, I never said she liked me back." Dan rebelled, but I blocked him out. "In fact, I think she might like someone else." I looked at Finn. "I just want her to be happy, you know? Even if it means I don't get to be with her."

Finn's brow creased, as if he couldn't comprehend how I could say this. "You really mean that?"

I nodded. It wasn't for Finn that I did it. It was for Cat. All her life she'd wanted to be accepted. Maybe this was a way I could give her that.

"I've never heard you talk like this about a girl before," said Finn.

"I've never felt like this about a girl before."

Trent came out, acting giddy and secretive. "Mission accomplished," he announced.

Finn and Trent joked on the way home, but I didn't say anything more. I didn't need to — the seeds had been planted. By the time I dropped them off, the sky had darkened and kids in costumes were going door-to-door, trick-or-treating. I locked myself in Dan's room and turned his music up to drown out the sound of the doorbell ringing.

Mission accomplished, I thought. I'd invited Cat to the party. I'd set it up so Finn would be interested in her. I'd paved the way for their storybook romance—the one Cat deserved to have. All that remained was to keep Dan from going to the party and wrecking everything.

Night

WTF R U?

I stared at the text from Trent. Then I checked the wall for the thirteenth time. *Don't go, don't go, don't go,* I whispered, turning the words into a mantra.

My control felt solid, but I wasn't about to take any chances. Dan might have stayed distant most of the day because I'd followed his desires. He wanted to drive Finn to school, and I'd done that. He wanted to ask Cat to the party, and I'd asked her. But staying home from the party was something I knew he'd fight me on.

Got caught sneaking out, I replied.

I read the message several times, only I couldn't think of any clever abbreviations for what I wanted to say. Hopefully the text would be enough to convince Trent to leave me alone. Getting caught seemed almost respectable. Never mind that it wasn't remotely true. Dan's mom had practically begged me to go out. "It's Halloween," she'd said, giving me a skeleton shirt she'd bought on her way home from work. "You used to love Halloween."

After sending the text, I paced Dan's room. I'd already unplugged his clocks to keep them from triggering Dan. Nevertheless, from the darkness outside, I figured it had to be after eight. If it were up to Dan, he would have been at the party by now. Cat might have even given up on him already. I wondered if she felt upset or relieved that he wasn't there. Finn might see her wandering alone and go comfort her—

I shook my head, scattering images of the party. Too late. Dan was already surging against me. All it would take was losing focus for an instant, and he'd find a gap and force me back. I had to be vigilant.

The doorbell rang. I froze and listened to make sure it wasn't someone Dan knew. Several trick-or-treaters had come earlier, but from the sound of it, these were a few late-night stragglers. Dan's mom commented on what clever ninjas and pirates they were as she passed out candy. Then the door closed and things grew quiet again.

My hands shook. I needed to do something, but there was nothing to do in Dan's room, and the longer I remained cooped up, the more restless he'd get.

I pulled on the skeleton shirt Dan's mom had bought him and shuffled to the living room. Teagan huddled at one end of the couch, watching a horror movie. Their mom sat at the other end, wearing a witch's hat and black gown. She cradled an orange plastic pumpkin in her lap, ready to spring into action if any more ninjas arrived.

"These contacts suck," said Teagan, rubbing her eyes. "I can't even see the TV."

"Good thing you have an eye appointment tomorrow," replied her mom.

Teagan scowled and kept fiddling with her contacts. She was always squinting and blinking and rubbing her eyes. Her comment gave me an idea.

I ducked into the garage before anyone saw me. If I filled up Dan's car now, then I wouldn't run out of gas tomorrow and Teagan wouldn't miss her eye appointment. Driving seemed out of the question, since it would bring Dan dangerously close to the party. But if I took the spare gas can, I could walk to the station on Main Street and fill it up. That seemed harmless enough, and it would keep me busy for an hour or more.

I checked the shelf for the red gas can that I'd used the

other day. The second shelf closest to the door—that's exactly where it had been. Or where it would be.

After a few minutes of searching, I spotted a red can by the lawn mower. It looked the same as the one I'd carried to the station, but when I picked it up, some liquid sloshed around. Strange. The can I'd used the other day had been empty. I unscrewed the cap and tilted the can.

Clear, slick fluid rushed out, coming faster than I'd anticipated. It splashed the lawn mower and stained the floor. Instantly, the garage filled with the heady reek of gasoline.

My thoughts skipped back to Cat's secret house. This same smell had been there the night of the fire. I hadn't recognized it then. The smell of candles and spray paint had covered it up, but now that I smelled the gas, I realized there was no mistaking it. When Dan had fallen near the couch, the thin fumes had made him dizzy. Parts of the couch must have been drenched in gasoline—that would explain why it burst into flames so easily. But who would pour gas on the couch?

Poor man's paint thinner, I thought, remembering the milk jug of gas Cat had brought to clean her brushes. She was the only one in the house before Finn arrived.

Why would Cat soak the couch in gasoline? She knew Finn was coming. She'd invited him. She'd even urged him to sit on the couch. I remembered her standing in front of him, holding a candle. *Tell me what I meant to you,* she said before Dan barged in.

Did she want the couch to burn? Was she trying to scare Finn? Or worse?

Stop lying! she told him.

My head spun. What if Dan hadn't raped Cat after all? What if it was someone else? Like Finn?

All at once, things I thought I knew began to shift. The subtle way Finn controlled everyone. His confidence and charm. What he'd said to Dan about not making a big deal out of things.

Cat's expression as she watched Finn flirt with Kendra in biology class came back to me. It wasn't jealousy sharpening her gaze. It was anger, because Finn always got away with things. And if Cat stayed silent, he'd keep getting away with things and hurt others like he'd hurt her. But what could she do? Who would believe her if she accused Finn?

That's why she invited him to the house. She tricked him into coming so she could get him to admit what he'd done. So she could finally stop him.

You ruined it, she'd told Dan the night of the fire.

And if he hadn't arrived, how far would she have taken things? How badly did Finn hurt her?

"Oh, God," I whispered, suddenly realizing what I'd done.

I checked Dan's cell phone. Ten till nine. Because of me, Cat might have been at Finn's house for nearly an hour by now. I rushed back to Dan's room to get his keys.

DON'T GO!

The words carved into the wall sent a chill down my spine. If I went to the party, things might turn out exactly as they had before. The only way to be certain of changing tracks was to stay here. But how could I if Cat was in trouble? It was my fault she'd gone to the party, and it would be my fault if Finn raped her.

I grabbed the keys and headed out.

The scent of gasoline in the garage made me want to vomit. Dan sensed my panic, but I was too focused on saving Cat to worry about him. I gripped the steering wheel and raced to Finn's house, driving through two stop signs and a red light. When I got there, I didn't bother to knock. Music blared and smoke curled around me as I barged through the front door.

"Shut the damn door," someone growled.

Several guys I didn't recognize were hunched over in the front room, passing a pipe. I pushed my way through the crowd and searched for Cat.

"Danny boy!" Dave clasped my arm, slurring his words. "You made it, dude. You got five dollars?"

"Where's Finn?"

"He's here. But you got to pay me five dollars first."

"I need to find someone."

"You still got to pay."

"I'll pay Finn later," I said.

Dave backed off, catching the anger in my voice.

The crowd appeared thickest near the kitchen. I cut through the press of bodies, ignoring people's grumbles and rude remarks. For once, Dan's height came in handy. I scanned the faces of people milling around the kegs in the kitchen, but I didn't see Cat. Or Finn.

I continued on to the living room. Orange Halloween lights dangled from the ceiling, and a strobe flashed while dance music shook the floor. My pulse raced, spurring Dan into a frenzy. I spotted Trent on the sofa drinking a beer.

"Look who escaped," he said. "About time you arrived."

"Have you seen Cat?"

"Who?"

I shouted my question again, thinking the music had drowned out my words.

Trent's gaze slipped over my shoulder.

"The girl we were talking about this morning," I said. "Is she here?"

"Dude, forget about her. She's not all that."

"Did you see her?"

"You get my text?" he answered.

"I'm not messing around, Trent."

"Then you should have been here when I texted you." Trent focused on someone beyond me. I turned to see who he was looking at. A few people danced in the center of the room. One of them was the guy Trent would kiss next week.

When I looked back, Trent gulped his beer.

"Tell me where she is, or I'll tell everyone you like him," I said.

Trent's face paled. He seemed about to deny it, but something in my expression must have convinced him otherwise. "I don't know, man," he said. "Maybe she went home. She looked pretty trashed."

"You saw her? When?"

"A half hour ago."

"Who was she with?"

He fiddled with his beer.

I grabbed Trent's collar. "Who was she with?"

"Finn," he said. "He took her upstairs. That's why I sent you the text. I was trying to warn you, jackass."

I bolted upstairs, too angry to think.

A few people cluttered the hallway, waiting for the bathroom. I edged past them and threw open the first door I came to. It led to a large bedroom with an empty canopy bed. The next room was locked. I tried the door at the end of the hall. The only light came from a computer screen, glowing blue. I flipped a switch and the bedside lamp blinked on.

Covers rustled as someone turned away from the light. Stepping closer, I made out Cat's jagged hair and smooth jaw. Her eyes were shut and the bedspread had tangled around her neck and limbs in an awkward way. It looked like she'd tried to pull the blankets around her, but she was on them instead of beneath them, so she couldn't keep herself covered.

"Cat?" I brushed her hair back. Her forehead felt damp.

Cat lifted her arm, but it flopped on the pillow. She kept her eyes shut and her face turned away. Then I noticed a button hanging from a thread. The vest she wore had been ripped open, and her bra was pushed up. I tugged it down, trying not to look at her chest.

The door rattled but no one came in. One of the drunk guys in the hall must have bumped against it. I reached beneath Cat's shoulders to carry her out. When I lifted her, the covers slid off and I saw that her pants were missing. Blood stained her underwear. I found her pants at the foot of the bed. I tried to push her feet into the leg holes, only it was hard to get her dressed without her help. Her head lolled from side to side, and she kicked weakly.

"What are you doing?" she muttered, eyes straining to open.

"I'm getting you out of here."

"Dan?"

"It's okay," I said, even though it wasn't okay. Nothing about this was okay. "I'm sorry. I should have been here."

She sat up, fighting against whatever drugs Finn had given her. Then her expression changed. "No," she said, pushing me back. "I don't want this."

She stumbled out of bed, but she couldn't get her shirt to stay closed. Several buttons were missing.

I reached for her.

"Don't touch me!" Her gaze flicked to a green top hat and velvet coat by the bed—part of her costume. The Mad Hatter. Her boots were there as well. She staggered into the hall, leaving her things behind.

"Cat!"

She kept going, barefoot and shirt open, down the stairs to the living room. People's eyes widened when they saw her. Some whistled or laughed.

"Looks like Danny boy got lucky after all," said Finn in a voice loud enough for half the room to hear. He grinned at me from the base of the stairs, but there was nothing friendly in his expression. Already, he was trying to shift the blame to Dan.

I grabbed his shirt. For an instant, Finn looked unsure of himself, then his confident, lazy smile slid back into place. "What's wrong?" he asked, lowering his voice so only I could hear. "Can't stand coming in second place for a change?"

I considered strangling him. Dan would have let me — he seemed to want to as much as I did.

"Get out of my way!" Cat shouted.

She was by the back sliding-glass door. Bella and Laney stood before her, blocking her exit. Bella held a phone, and she was snapping pictures and taunting Cat, telling her to "work it." I tossed Finn aside and shoved through the room to help her. Then she was out, running barefoot across the yard. I followed her down the block, still thinking that if only I could catch her, I might be able to fix things. It wasn't until Cat turned onto a side street and the party faded into the distance that I realized I was the reason she kept running.

I slowed and called her name one last time, but she didn't stop. The petal-white bottoms of her feet flickered into the darkness between houses.

Did she think I'd attacked her? Or was she simply too hurt to come back?

Either way it didn't matter because now I could see, with perfect clarity, what I'd done. Instead of changing things, I'd made them happen. I'd caused what I'd feared, and now Cat was gone.

I turned my back on the lights of the neighborhood. The dark spiderweb structure of the train trestle loomed less than a block away. For once I didn't try to run from my fate. When I reached the train trestle, I walked along the tracks until I stood above the river. Things had come full circle.

I'd thought knowing the future would make a difference, but it's no different from knowing the past. Only the present matters, and I'd acted no better in mine than Dan had in his. All that was left was to be hit on the head. Was it a stranger who would do it? Or Finn? Or someone else?

I didn't fear getting injured. Not anymore. I'd already failed Cat, Teagan, Dan's mom and dad, and everyone else who knew him. With every decision I'd made, I'd made things worse. I deserved this.

"I'm here!" I yelled into the darkness. "Come on, hit me."

In response, all I heard was the trickle of water over the rocks below.

I searched the shadows for my attacker, but no one came. There was just me, standing on a bridge over a river. My chest felt hollow. It had been me all along. I'd invited Cat to the party. I'd gotten Finn interested in her. I'd set her up to be raped. And then I'd abandoned her. *I* was the problem—the thing that was wrong. Not Dan. *Me.*

I peered over the edge of the bridge, wishing there was

some way I could go back and erase everything I'd done. The ground where the zombie would wake tomorrow, dizzy and bleeding, lay directly beneath me. A short, bitter laugh escaped my throat as I realized what I had to do.

I climbed over the bridge railing.

Dan resisted, but I pushed him back and leaned away from the railing. The ground bristled with rocks.

Maybe I'd fall and hit my head, and everything would be exactly as it had been before. Dan would wake up tomorrow beneath the bridge with a wound on his forehead and a deep, destructive self-hatred. Or maybe this time, when I fell, things would be different. This could be the lever I'd been searching for. All I had to do was lean a little more to change how I landed. An inch could mean the difference between life and death. Hit a rock headfirst and it would all be over—Dan and I would both be removed from the equation.

I took a deep breath and let go of the railing.

Dan resisted, but I shut him out and kept leaning. My muscles twitched, and my body tilted farther from the bridge. I focused all my will on this one thing—leaning until my control shattered.

Instantly, Dan shoved me aside and took over. He twisted. Hands reached back for the bridge railing. Fingertips brushed wood. Too late. Gravity had claimed him. His feet broke free of the ledge. Arms flailed, useless, through the air. And then we were falling. Cartwheeling through the night sky.

Dan's frantic thoughts mixed with my own. It surprised me how much he wanted to live. I saw his body in the tub. The note he'd left his sister. How he'd tried to protect Cat by following her into her secret house. The hero he wanted so badly to be.

We hit the ground with a bone-jarring impact. His knees collapsed, and his hands shot out to fend off rocks. Then his chest came down, and last his head, smacking a fallen log. A tidal wave of pain broke over me. I didn't try to hold on anymore. Instead, I let go. I let Dan's fear and rage and hurt carry me away.

His eyes flickered shut and senses swirled like the last drops of water spinning into a drain as he blacked out. I followed the water down, surrendering myself completely.

Funny, I thought. *I'd despised Dan for killing himself, and here I was doing the same thing — trying to end my existence.*

In that moment, I finally understood him. How much he hurt. How deeply he cared. How noble and flawed we both were.

Friday,
October 31

I woke up drowning. The undertow of time pulled me farther from shore, increasing in strength with each passing second. There was no going back. No land to cling to. No returning to myself. There was only the question of how long I'd have before I slipped under and what my last moment of awareness would be.

Things came in flashes and stutters. I knew immediately that it was Friday morning again—the day of the Halloween party. It had never occurred to me before how different the light was every morning. The subtle changes in the smell of each day. The ever-evolving symphony of birds, wind, and leaves. I'd taken these things for granted, but the moment Dan opened his eyes, I knew this was the same day I'd lived before. The tide of time had shifted.

Perhaps it's like this for everyone in the end—even if we want to die, we fight it. I thought of how Dan had struggled in the tub to hold on before taking his final breath and letting go. And how, on the bridge, his hands had shot out for something solid to grab on to. We cling to what we know.

I suppose that's why, as I faded into him, I clung to all that I'd done and seen. My time may have been short, but it was still my life—everything I'd been bound up in two backwards weeks. I sorted the days into a story I could tell myself, like a book written in disappearing ink, each word doomed to vanish shortly after I wrote it.

And the end of my story? Here's what I saw:

A mirror. The familiar brushing of teeth. The shower with its blissful abundance of water. A sense of melting. A fleeting notion that to be nothing is to be boundless.

Dan dried himself. Dressed. It was so hard to separate my being from his anymore.

Back in his room, he lifted the calendar off the wall and turned the page from this month to the next. Then he stared at the blank spot where the calendar had hung.

I considered encouraging him to write a message there. Something inspirational like THERE IS ONLY NOW.

That seemed a funny thing to carve beneath a calendar. But then I decided, or he decided, it would be better to leave it blank. Leave things open to possibility. Maybe he could hang some pictures on the wall to brighten the room. He might even paint them himself.

"You still thinking about Thanksgiving?" asked his sister from the doorway. She tried to sound neutral, but her anxiety about him leaving was obvious.

He tossed the calendar onto his bed. "I think I might stick around," I said. Or he said. "That is, if it's okay with you?"

"That's great." She smiled, then caught herself and put on a more stern expression. "As long as you don't eat all the mashed potatoes."

I lost track of things for a while after that, my awareness diffusing like blood in a stream.

His phone buzzed with a text. Someone named Finn wanted to be picked up. I tried to recall who that was, but my memories flowed away from me. All I could come up with was a vague sense of irritation at the tone of the message.

Mom asked if he'd take Teagan to school.

He looked at his sister, and she tensed. She seemed ready to storm out. I pictured the small cracks gradually widening, becoming insurmountable chasms. And so I said, "Yes."

He said, "Yes."

That seemed important, although I couldn't remember why anymore.

When his phone rang again, he turned it off, ignoring Finn's second text.

Teagan got into the car. He started the engine and drove down leaf-covered streets. She complained about not having a chance to eat breakfast. "Let's get some donuts," she said, pointing to a gas station. "I'll run in. It'll only take a second."

He pulled into the station and parked by one of the pumps. While she was gone, the smell of gas caught his attention. He glanced at the dash. The tank was nearly empty.

Better fill it up, I thought. *Take care of what you can.*

He unhooked the nozzle and refueled his car. This, too, felt different. This mattered.

"I got Bavarian cream for you," said Teagan, returning with a white paper bag. "That's your favorite, right?"

At school he stayed in his car to eat the donuts with his sister.

Students gathered in clusters around the main doors. A girl wearing striped leggings stood by the flagpole talking with a large girl dressed in black. Teagan zipped up her backpack, preparing to join them.

"Are those your friends?" he asked her.

"Maybe." She sounded surprised that he cared. I don't think he'd ever asked her this before. "They're juniors. Do you know them?"

He shook his head. "Not really. I'd like to meet them sometime. They seem nice."

"They are," she said. "Especially Cat. You'd love her."

I smiled, knowing his sister was right. I would love her. So would he. And someday he'd tell her as much.

The first bell rang. People began to shuffle inside. Teagan stepped out and hurried after them.

He watched her go.

I watched, raising a hand to wave at the girl in the striped leggings. She paused and waved back. Whether she was waving to him or to me, I couldn't tell. In that moment, everything felt connected. Whole.

It's time, I thought, unable to cling to my separateness any longer.

This was it. The tale had caught up to the telling. The words disappeared as I thought them. The last memory of my self vanished.

And then—

Gold leaves against a blue sky.

The smell of apples and smoke in the air.

A girl with a scar above her lip looking back and smiling.

A taste of sweetness on my tongue.

"Life can only be understood backwards; but it must be lived forwards."

—Søren Kierkegaard

ACKNOWLEDGMENTS

A few years ago a woman wrote me a letter in which she thanked me for writing *The Secret to Lying* because it helped her understand her son better—her son who killed himself when he was eighteen. That letter deeply saddened me. It also changed me. I hadn't considered *The Secret to Lying* to be a book about suicide, but receiving that letter helped me realize the necessity for writers to take risks and grapple with difficult issues. Without the courage and honesty of that woman, and others like her who are brave enough to risk sharing their stories of loss, bullying, and sexual assault, this book would not exist.

I'm also grateful to all the friends, family, and editors who helped me untie the many knots that formed in my head as I was working on this book. Special thanks go to:

Jen Yoon, for seeing the heart of the story and for taking the time to push me at least three drafts beyond what I would have done on my own.

Ginger Knowlton, for being an incredible agent and all-around excellent human being. Knowing you makes me happy.

The fabulous folks at Candlewick Press, for believing in this book. I especially want to thank Liz Bicknell, for editing some of my all-time favorite authors and deciding to take a chance on me. Carter Hasegawa for always being in touch and shepherding this book through several copyedits (sorry about those last-minute changes). Erin DeWitt for being an incredible copyeditor. Hannah Mahoney for her considerable copyediting skills. Nathan Pyritz for the creative interior design. Kathryn Cunningham for the alluring jacket design. And all the other fine folks at Candlewick who work tirelessly to publish some of the best books in the business.

My writing partners, especially Laura Resau, Amy Kathleen Ryan, Victoria Hanley, Trai Cartwright, and Lauren Sabel for giving me advice, encouragement, and support (while also writing kick-ass books that I love to read).

My fellow teachers at Colorado State University who've supported my writing.

Cloud Cult, Sigur Rós, and Iron and Wine, for the music that kept me going on this one.

My parents and my sister, for constant support and much-needed vacations. Marc and Nancy Eglin, for the summer writing retreat. And my daughters, Addison and Cailin, for reminding me of what matters most every day.

Finally, I want to thank my wife, Kerri, for reading this more times than I can count, being both muse and creator, and for keeping me from floating away. You are the little light in the sparkling neighborhood below who calls me back to earth.

Whatever you're going through, there are people who want to listen and support you. Here are just a few places you might visit or call:

National suicide lifeline: 1-800-273-TALK
www.suicidepreventionlifeline.org

To Write Love on Her Arms
www.twloha.com

RAINN (Rape, Abuse and Incest National Network):
1-800-656-HOPE
www.rainn.org

www.stopbullying.gov

Call, speak out, take a risk, and take action. You are not alone.